VOIDED

By Ace Parlier

Published by The Elite Lizzard Publishing Company

Acknowledgements

This book was inspired, in large part, by a writing exercise devised by my good friend, and a true force of nature, Zorha Redwolf Edwards.

I'd also like to thank Anne Leigh Parrish for her encouragement as I labored over the first draft.

And to my children, Keagan, Thomas, Cierra and Charles, and my grandchildren, Dalton, Leo, Elizabeth, Joslyn, and Serenity; Not a day goes by when you're not in my thoughts. You are a constant source of inspiration and joy.

I love you all!

This book is dedicated to the memory of my mother.

Brenda Kay Parlier

(1947-2021)

Chapter 1

"Nena Videt, stand and await transfer."

The lights inside my cell activated as the canned command blared in my ears. I snapped awake, disoriented, but not surprised. I suspected the Navy would be back around to visit. The rumor going up and down the columns was that Olankampf had been voided.

They needed another sucker to go down the Well.

I rubbed my eyes, yawning, as I stepped into the dresser. This would be my tenth drop, a record, if I survived.

There was no shortage of fodder available to make the drop through hyperspace. There were hundreds of pilots of varying skill in this prison facility alone. But Magister Lopast took some sort of twisted pleasure in sending me, especially after someone voided. I must have reminded her of an old, despised girlfriend or something.

She had a soft spot for me.

As soon as I was dressed, snug in my suppression jumper, I took my place with my back to the hatch and waited for the guards to descend.

From my place at the bottom of my column, there wasn't a lot to see besides the dull mottled green disk of Caelus, the gas giant we orbited. It was a breathtaking view, one that enchanted me when I first arrived. But, after a decade suspended above it in my polymer cage, it became another sickening reminder of a world I'd never see again.

After a few seconds, the hatch opened, and I was guided backwards into the lift. I concentrated on being as pliant as possible as I was pulled along. The guards here took zero risks when interacting with prisoners. If I'd so much as twitch, they would activate the jumpsuit, crushing me to the point of possible asphyxiation. It was completely their call at that point whether you lived or died. No one questioned their decisions.

No one up top cared.

The galaxy's most dangerous dregs were abandoned here, stacked in twenty-foot diameter pods that formed helical columns hanging in rows around the lower perimeter of the facility. As far as Union prisons went, it wasn't a bad place. I had seen some of their dirtside prisons that far surpassed the inhumane.

The lift opened to the holding station at the top of my column. There, two more guards waited to escort me for the ride up to Administration. Inside the secured lift, you could see half of the station as it ascended the outer hull.

It was as wondrous as it was depressing. Still, it was nice to be out of my cell and moving, even if it was toward my own destruction. After all this time I'd learned to be grateful for small deviations from the norm.

The worst thing about Eridani Pier was the total lack of personal interaction. Once you were locked into your pod that was it. That's where you stayed.

Virtual interaction was available on the prison meta-network, but it was a freak show that I avoided. The only worthwhile thing on the 'net was access to the library of the galaxy's music. There, I discovered music from worlds that I'd only heard of in legends.

That was my bliss.

The Union of Galactic Commerce may have been a lot of terrible things, but it stood firm on its principle of plurality. The home space culture turned on the trends and trinkets brought back by the ambassador caravans. But, sometimes, those same caravans brought back war.

The latest and greatest one had led me here

Magister Britva Lopast stared mirthlessly as her assistant took custody of me from the guards. The hybrid showed me politely to a chair then walked quickly away. Across the room, a human fleet admiral sat with a drink in his hand.

His presence caught me off guard. The Union had never sent an admiral to collect me before. It was usually some wet-behind-the-ears Tech Corp ensign, scared that I would bite them.

"Well, Videt, I'm sure you know why you're here," Lopast smirked, tugging at the tunic of her stiff gray uniform.

"And a fair good morning to you as well, Madame Magister. It's nice to see you again."

Across the room, the admiral chuckled. Lopast frowned, making the deep lines in her ancient face look even more rugged.

"I'm here because you're ready to dump me down the Well again." I shifted in my seat, staring her dead in the eye. "Someone said Olankampf had been voided."

Lopast scowled. She loathed information leaks inside the prison. But, in all the years I'd been here she hadn't managed to cut off the source. And I couldn't help baiting her.

I relished the interaction.

"He was." She sat down at her desk, casting a derisive eye my way. "His was the first drop in a new Well. Something went wrong."

"So now you need another dummy." I sat forward in my seat.

The sudden movement caused Lopast to grab for the pad controlling my jumpsuit.

I smiled. I loved that I made her nervous. "I take it you've fixed the malfunction?"

The admiral stood and crossed the room. "We suspect the accident was due to pilot error rather than any kind of technical glitch. The conditions inside this new Well are quite different from the one at Starbow. Olankampf couldn't adapt."

"What makes you think I'll fare any better? Hyperspace may just be too wild there. I've seen it before."

The admiral frowned. He wasn't used to people questioning him. "Magister Lopast assured me you were a more accomplished pilot."

I glanced at Lopast arching an eyebrow. *Oh, I just bet she did.*

Up close, the Admiral, Kirpich, wasn't a bad looking man. He was older, probably in his nineties. He was distinguished, tall and lanky with salt and pepper hair. His hands were heavily scarred, burnt, as if he'd been forged in the fire of battle. He had a commanding presence.

Given the opportunity, I'd take him for a ride.

Or, perhaps, I'd been here too long.

"Do you have all of Olankampf's data? Simulating the conditions is really the only thing that will help."

As I spoke, it dawned on me that I was being sucked right back into that calculated mode of thinking. The military had destroyed my life.

And, after they did that, they expected me to go on trying to kill myself for free.

Which, given the alternative, I was willing to do.

I couldn't spend the rest of my life here.

"We only have partial data," the general sat down in the chair beside me, facing me. "The readings skew in the moments leading up to signal loss."

As I listened, I noticed the *Space*, *Air* and *Surface* insignia on his sleeve. I found it suspicious that a special forces admiral would be overseeing a Tech Corp project.

Perhaps the war wasn't going as well as the propaganda suggested.

I let out a long, slow, cleansing breath as I organized my thoughts.

"If I do this, I want time off of my sentence."

The words escaped my lips.

Lopast pointed a skeletal finger at me. "You are in no position to bargain, Videt. This is not a negotiation. You will do as ordered, or-.

The Admiral held up a hand, cutting Lopast off. He stared at me for an eye blink before smiling. "I'll do you one better. I need a total of three runs made. If you survive them all, I'll commute your sentence."

"What? That's not what we discussed." Lopast croaked like she'd swallowed a bug.

The Admiral scowled, "You behave as if you are able to bargain as well, Magister. I came here to collect Commander Videt. Your assistance in the matter has ended."

Lopast lurched from her chair. Her skeletal frame moved at awkward angles as she crossed the room to scowl out of the viewport. It was rumored that everything below her skull was synthetic.

I believed it of her heart.

"I've read your file, Commander Videt. I know what happened at Almawti. I have a Captain under my command you might remember, Gevin Toll?"

I glanced at the admiral and laughed, but underneath I was fighting tears. "Toll is a Captain? I figured he'd be on Parasaam cataloging plant species by now."

The Admiral smiled. "If he had his way, he would be. He still has a couple more years before he can retire." He stared me dead in the eye as he rested his hand on my leg. I smiled. It was the most action I'd had in years.

"So, are you in, Commander?"

I shrugged. "Well, the odds are stacked against me. But it's worth it to finally be rid of our learned Magister, one way or the other."

Lopast glared but didn't speak. She'd miss me.

"When do we leave?" I asked.

The Admiral paused, gazing at me with what I imagined to be an admiring look, or, he could have just been horny. I hadn't known him long enough to tell.

I was fine with it, either way.

“I’ll have you taken to my ship as soon as they remove you from that cowardly nanite contraption.”

I looked across at Lopast flashing my most wicked grin. “At your leisure, Magister, but, if I were you, I wouldn’t keep the Admiral waiting.”

Admiral Kirpich’s flagship, the *Shaytan,* was a marvel of Union technology. I stood at the viewport dumbfounded as we ferried out. It was flattened ovoid, at least 8 kilometers long, with real-space and hyper-wave engines trailing behind it. Amidship, the command tower rose to the height of a twenty-story building and stretched the width and half the length of the ship.

It was a city floating in space.

“By the Ancients, that’s a big ship.”

“It is a sight to see, isn’t it?” Kirpich joined me at the viewport.

He dismissed his personal guard before they followed him across the narrow width of the ferry. Even so, they continued to study my every move.

I was, after all, a Pier con and not to be trusted.

"I've never seen anything like it. When did they push that thing out of the shipyard?"

I saw the Admiral's grin reflected in the viewport, "About five standard years after they built a facility big enough to contain it. I was assigned to her before she hit hard vacuum. She's only been in service a few months now."

"No wonder you need so much hyper-matter. I bet it takes a quarter of a kilogram just to get that big bitch moving."

The Admiral didn't reply. A flash of concern passed across his face.

"Is that why the Union built the second Well?" I turned from the viewport to look at him, "To power a fleet of these monsters?"

"You know I can't answer that, Commander."

I decided not to press my luck. I turned back to watch the ferry pass into the ship's shadow.

"The war is not going well," Karpich stepped closer, out of earshot of his guards. "We've ceded space all along the interior Arm. We're throwing everything we have at the Aratan perimeter soon. We need all the power we can muster."

I glanced at him sidelong. “So, I won’t need to brush up on my Aratani then, right?”

Kirpich grinned, studying the reflection of my face, “Not if you make my delivery, Commander.”

“I’m not sure anyone will make it if conditions are as unstable as you say.”

The Admiral put his hand in the small of my back, guiding me to a bench just past the viewport. “I wouldn’t call it unstable, exactly, but it is different. The readings, to the best that I can understand them, indicate a thicker, swifter moving current. I liken it to a swiftly moving river rather than waves against the shore.”

I smirked imagining it. “I can see why it’d be hard to drop through. There’s probably a lot more density between slipstreams.”

Kirpich nodded, “That was the summation given to your Olankampf before his drop. My Corp Commander saw the need for a different strategy, so we modified the dropships to adapt.”

“Heavier Shields?”

“With a fine-tuned shaping ability. Look, Commander, all the cards on the table, it is dangerous, but I don’t think it’s impossible. My Corp Commander is a mad genius. If he says his ship will make it, it will.”

I investigated Kirpich's eyes. His confidence in his crew was admirable. He seemed the example of an old school officer, kind, upholding of the Tenets. I could have thrived under his command.

"Well, I'd sure as hell like to make it."

The Admiral laughed loudly. "As I can well imagine. You have Captain Toll to thank for the opportunity. He was the one that discovered you were flying drops at Starbow. Once he told me the whole story of you and Captain Cray, I agreed to look into it."

"Gevin was my right hand for years. He's a good man. Loyal."

The Admiral nodded. "And any officer that inspires that kind of loyalty deserves a second chance. Those are the type of Mariners I pick for my crew."

"I'll do my best, sir. That's all I've got."

The gentle nudge of *Shaytan's* docking control brought the ferry to a stop. I followed the Admiral aft to the hatch as the guards fell in behind.

The Admiral's hybrid attaché met us at the hatch. As with the ship, it was a brand-new model I hadn't seen before. It looked real. The depth in its eyes was unsettling. If not for the tag tattooed on its cheek, I'd have never guessed it wasn't sentient.

After it helped fit the Admiral's command crown, Kirpich nodded at me, "Viginti, this is Commander Nena Videt. She is on temporary assignment as a liaison to the Well project with full privileges as befits her rank. See that she is logged in, fed, and fitted for uniform."

Beside me, I saw one of the guards do a double take. Just like that, I was their superior officer. I looked at the Admiral questioningly.

He arched an eyebrow. "I can trust you, right?"

"Yes, sir." I saluted.

The Admiral smiled returning my salute, "Report to me in the Engineering Lab in three hours standard, Commander."

I did my damnedest not to grin like a fool, "Three standard, sir, mark."

"Dismissed."

I followed the hybrid aft walking on air. I knew this stunt was only a lateral move. I wasn't free. But I was a hell of a lot better off than I was stuck in stir over Caelus.

Now all I had to do was stay alive.

Chapter 2

I followed the hybrid to a turbo tram, studying her as we stepped inside. She was flawless. And built a little too anatomically correct for my taste. I didn't know if that spoke to the Admiral's proclivities or my own pagan distrust.

"Do we have far to go?"

Viginti smiled, taking a seat. She patted the spot next to her. "Get comfortable, Commander. We have a ten-minute ride aft. You're birthed with flight command personnel."

"Back in the Hive. Nice!"

"Hive?" Viginti's face went blank. Creepy

"Sorry. It's what pilots call the command quarters. Everyone's a bad ass, ready to strike on a moment's notice. It's like a beehive."

"Beehive." Viginti considered the word.

Apparently, the Admiral liked them stacked and stupid.

"Okay, let's just move on. How far is the Engineering Lab from there?"

"A short ride down and fore. The Engineering Lab is above the main hanger. Your attaché is prepared with everything you'll need to adapt to your new post, Commander."

"Attaché?" I didn't like the sound of it.

"All command level staff are assigned an administrative assistant. I might not know anything about beehives, Commander, but I do know you throttle jockeys are terrible about posting reports."

"Touché."

"I may not know everything, Commander, but I know everything I need to do my job."

"My apologies."

Great, a hybrid with feelings. It didn't seem like a good idea.

"Your personnel file says you're from Janus."

"I am." I frowned, wondering her intent. "My father was the Union Ambassador."

"Not a popular title on your world."

I shot the hybrid a sidelong glance wondering how angry the Admiral would be if I disassembled her.

"A necessary evil, as my father would say."

"Well, I can certainly understand why you're not comfortable with hybrids, then." Viginti's gaze held a perilous depth.

It was wholly disconcerting.

"You're right. My father refused to have them around. I didn't see one up close until I arrived at the Naval Academy. Back then, they were easy to spot."

I gave Viginti the once over. "The technology has come a long way. If not for your scan code, I'd never been able to tell."

A flash of emotion passed across Viginti's face.

"Another necessary evil, I'm afraid. The rules have changed during your incarceration, Commander. I can't go into detail per the admiral's orders but, long story short, I'm as flesh and blood as you."

I found the idea terrifying and the ramifications more so.

"Then why are you branded as property? That's immoral."

"Because of the cybernetics. My synaptic net is still heuristic in nature, but the carrier medium is chemical instead of electronic."

"So, the Union won't afford you full rights. That's deplorable."

Viginti rose from her seat. She looked away at the streaking lights outside the tram tube. "If we don't win this war, Commander, it won't matter. The way things are now, I'm not sure the Union will survive a victory. It's a mess out there."

I stared at her as the enormity of her statement registered. "Looks like I'm entirely out of the loop."

Viginti smiled. It was faint but genuine. "You'll have plenty of time to catch up on the flight out.

The Admiral didn't want you bombarded on your first day. Your mission is vital, Commander. If it were me, I'd focus on that. The shitstorm can wait."

I grinned. She sounded like every other Mariner I'd ever known

"The shitstorm always awaits."

I worried about what Viginti had said as I made my way to the Engineering Lab. I had plenty of time. It took me twenty minutes to commute there from my assigned berth. I was glad I skipped the meal and headed out early.

Back in my old life, before the conviction, I would tour each new ship I was assigned to, to get a sense of it, a sense of the crew and the rhythm it operated under. As I looked around the *Shaytan* I realized it was impossible. There were just too many moving parts. Admiral Kirpich had to inspire fanatic loyalty to keep this floating city on point.

It was a lot to manage.

The Engineering Lab was as big as the main hanger. It rose the height of several decks and had its own launch bays. I had no clue where to look for the Corp Commander. It was like exploring a whole new neighborhood.

I hustled across the deck checking out all the equipment parked in various states of disrepair. There was a lot of hardcore armor on board. The *Shaytan* seemed poised to drop a whole lot of heavy metal dirtside.

"Can I help you, Commander?"

A hybrid dressed in greasy gray coveralls stepped out from the engine hatch of a landing ring. He was an older model, not manufactured to look like any species.

This one really creeped me out.

“I’m looking for the Commander’s office?”

Just then, another being, an Etherai, stuck its head out of the hatch. “Why do you need to see the Commander?”

I glared, taking umbrage with his tone. “I’m reporting for duty, and you are whom exactly?

As far as I knew, Etherai weren’t permitted in the Union Navy. They were an allied species but not part of the Union. I guessed that status had changed.

“I’m Commander Nalwist. Now, why would I have a pilot reporting for duty? I need technicians.”

Nalwist climbed out of the hatch and dropped down staring at me curiously.

Etherai were a flightless avian species. They reminded me of egg hens in the way they gawked at you. They were fidgety and always on the move. That this was the genius engineer Admiral Kirpich vaunted shook my faith in him. Etherai were usually flaky.

“I’m here to fly the next Well drops. I’ve just arrived with Admiral Kirpich.”

Nalwist's eyes shot open wide with surprise. "Oh, Oh, yes! You're the Captain's friend! I've heard about you. Please, Commander, follow me."

I followed Nalwist to a lift station as he prattled on about the Well project. I tried to keep up with his chatter, but it was too much to process.

Inside his briefing room, a freaky pair of Corp techs busied themselves preparing for the meeting.

A hologram of the dropship floated over the conference table that dominated the center of the room.

When Kirpich said he needed more power he wasn't kidding. The raw power of three of these tankers full of hyper-matter was enough to destroy an entire star system. The thought of towing one up through hyperspace was unsettling.

"Commander Videt, these are Lieutenants Lam and Taito. They built your new dropship.

I returned their salute absently while soaking information from the display. "It's a whole hell of a lot bigger than the pods I flew at Starbow."

"We need to make the most out of the drops we make." Nalwist skittered in place. "We cannot risk keeping the Well open for long."

"Because of the conditions?"

"Because of its proximity to the Aratan frontier."

Admiral Kirpich, along with several members of his staff, entered and found places along the length of the table.

Captain Toll wasn't among them.

The Admiral sat at the head of the table and motioned for me to take the chair to his left. "That is why time is at a premium, Commander. We must complete our task as quickly and as quietly as possible."

"The system in which we'll place the Well had the most stable readings of anywhere in the sector." Nalwist touched the pad on his wrist-top and a map of the sector appeared over the table.

"I understand that hyperspace there is still pretty wild." I tilted my head trying to look the bird in the eye.

Nalwist shot me a twitchy sidelong glance. "It is less so than any of the other deep points we've charted. There were also issues of placement that had to be worked out with the Antithesians and conditions at their entry points."

"The who?" I glanced at the Admiral. "Who in hell are the Antithesians?"

Kirpich glanced at Nalwist who seemed suddenly repentant. "Well Chief, since you're the one to spill the fasol, you get to explain it to her."

Nalwist glanced unsteadily around, embarrassed, though it was hard to tell given an Etherai's inherent awkwardness.

"The Antithesians are the name given to the beings that inhabit the antithetical universe at the far side of the hyperspace layer.

I smirked, "Okay, now you're just messing with me, right?"

Kirpich shook his head, "I'm afraid not, Commander. We've been in contact with them for well over a decade. The ability to make the exchanges, however, wasn't possible until the last couple of years.

"So, am I supposed to dock with one of their ships? That's not what I did at Starbow."

"The procedure you followed at Starbow is the same thing you'll be doing here. You were led to believe that you were siphoning hyper-matter out of the Equispanse directly, were you not?" Kirpich asked.

"Uh-yeah," I looked around the room, "No one at Starbow ever said a thing to me about any Antithesians."

"Actually, Commander, you were better off not knowing." Kirpich stole another quick glance at Nalwist. "The siphoning process is an exchange with one of their ships through an induced negative space. If your matter and their antimatter came into direct contact, you would both be vaporized instantly as well as blowing a hell of a hole in hyperspace."

"So much so that it would disrupt galactic travel for years." Nalwist tilted his head considering it. "The hyperspace beacons in the entire sector would come unmoored like buoys in a hurricane."

I winked at the Admiral. "No pressure there."

"Don't overthink it, Commander. You've done an excellent job so far with inferior equipment. You'll have the better part of a week to study the data and get acquainted with your new ship. Just fly your mission and you'll be fine."

I faked my best smile, "Yes, sir."

"Now, if there isn't anything else, I'll leave you to get started." Admiral Kirpich rose, his staff following in unison. "Nalwist, get Commander Videt fitted with a command crown as soon as possible. I want her in a simulator first thing in the morning."

"Yes, sir. I can do it now. I'm sure the commander would like to see her ship."

"Yes, I would." I smiled.

"Excellent." Kirpich returned our salute. "And, Commander Videt, I would be honored if you would join Captain Toll and I for dinner this evening?"

"Absolutely, Admiral. I'd be honored."

"Good. 1800 sharp, Commander. Bring your appetite."

"Yes, sir."

Nalwist stared at me agog as the Admiral and his staff left the room. "An invitation to dinner? Not bad for your first day."

"I guess not. But he probably figures I won't be around long anyway, so he might as well seize the opportunity while it's available."

Nalwist snorted. "You worry too much, Commander. This drop ship is state of the art. I think you'll get through this just fine."

"I sure hope so. I've grown quite fond of living."

I followed Nalwist out of the conference room and into the lab. Inside Lam and Taito were tinkering with what I assumed to be my command crown.

Tech Corp technicians were their own sub-species. It didn't matter what world they were from, they all, little by little, merged with the technology they created. Lam and Taito were no different.

I wasn't sure yet which was who, but both were heavily modified to conduct their job aboard ship. The one holding the crown's entire left arm was a nanite tool replicator. He was downloading information into the crown through an interface currently replacing his index finger

The other one, who was slightly taller and surlier looking, was preparing the interlink that would interface directly with my smart-ass Janusian brain.

I sat down on a stool close to the second one pulling my hair up so he could insert the link into the tiny port at the base of my skull.

There is an 'aha' moment, when the interlink connects to the viscera of consciousness, where the whole of reality seems but a selfish dream. The world falls completely away, and the wisdom of the universe calls directly, illusion pulled fully aside to gaze at endless peace.

It is an immense instant of total bliss and entirely too fleeting.

I opened my eyes to find Nalwist leaning over me, panicking.

I leaped off the stool pushing him aside and keeping his technicians in front of me.

“Why are you in my face?”

“We were afraid you suffered an injury.” Nalwist scampered back out of arm’s reach. “You were out for several moments.”

“I always bliss out when I get jacked in. It’s no big deal.”

“It is common, but I’ve never seen it last that long.”

Taito and Lam shook their heads.

“I’m fine. I’ll be fine. It’s been a while since I ran a system. I just need to get back in the groove.”

“I think you should report to medical before we fit the crown. The rush of data could be damaging.” Nalwist’s tilted his head, turning his big ostrich eye my way.

I glared at the skittish little shit and thought about drop kicking him. I turned to the technician who inserted the link. “Can you compress the data stream and ramp it up in stages?”

The technician nodded then glanced at Nalwist.

“That may well be insufficient, Commander. The initial signal could be damaging. I don’t want to have to report to the Admiral that we fried your brain. This mission is too important.”

I understood his trepidation, I just wasn’t crazy about it. “Okay, how about this, get a med tech down here and have them run a holo-encephalograph while we ramp up the crown. I’ve seen that done before.”

Nalwist nodded. “True. But I can’t order that. That’ll have to come from the Admiral or Captain Toll. They need to be in the loop on this.”

“Yeah and Dr. Gillomi is a right pain in the ass about these things, too,” this from the tech adjusting the crown.

“Lieutenant Lam!” Nalwist shouted, more surprised than angry.

I smiled at Lam then turned to Nalwist. “Ah, a clearer view. You’re afraid of the doctor. Well, that’s great.”

Nalwist became flustered. He glared at Lam. It was more comical than threatening. “I am not afraid of Dr. Gillomi. But she can be quite difficult to deal with at times.”

"I'm sure." I grinned. "Being the Chief Medical Officer on this tug has got to be a headache. Well, do what you must, Commander. I'm going to nab a bite to eat. Hit me up when you're ready to proceed. I want to be in that ship tomorrow."

Nalwist blinked in response. I think he was finding me difficult to deal with as well.

"As soon as the Admiral is apprised things will move quickly. He doesn't like to be kept waiting, either."

"Excellent! Then I will see you shortly. Don't let these two nap while I'm gone."

Lam and Taito both grinned as I headed for the hatch.

Chapter 3

I made my way up to the main mess hall more than a little freaked out about the screw up with the data link. I was skating the edge of insubordination by bugging out on Nalwist and the boys, but I really needed to stretch my legs and clear my head.

It had been a hell of a day so far.

The mess hall turned out to be another of the *Shaytan's* surprises. It was a cavernous room terraced three decks high with honest to goodness kitchens serving real food. At least twenty different worlds were represented along with a few varied varieties thereof.

After a decade of multi-colored nutrient mush, I wept.

Then, after arguing with a hybrid chef over the proper interval to grill paper fish, I sat down alone with my tray and took in the whole mad scene.

The thing that struck me was the predominance of beings on the crew that were from home space. There wasn't the diversity one found on most Union ships. I couldn't remember seeing anyone that wasn't originally from Sector One.

I wondered if the crew wasn't a reflection of Kirpich's views on duty and loyalty. Which, I supposed, was his prerogative after surviving thirty years of constant war.

My choices might not have been that much different.

"That's her right there, Kirpich's latest project. And a convict no less."

I turned to see one of Kirpich's guards talking to a group of Marines a few tables behind me. He was the one that did the double take when Kirpich reinstated me. He didn't look pleased with the Admiral's decision.

I thought about smiling with a small debutante wave but decided against it. I didn't need new trouble. So, I carried on with my paper fish and pondered my rusty uplink. Until the big numbskull decided to stop by my table for a visit.

"So, what's your malfunction, convict? How'd you get on the Admiral's leash?"

I smirked. I couldn't help it. I cast my gaze directly into his right eye in a show of dominance. My grin widened as I pushed my tray away.

"That's Commander Convict to you, Gunny. You were there when I was reactivated, right?"

The Gunnery Sergeant's face cinched up in what looked like painful displeasure. He was wound tight.

"And if the Admiral wanted to share the circumstances of my mission with you, he'd have done so. So, I dare not go against his wishes on the matter."

The funny gunny snarled. He was a formidable being. Human but no doubt with Tabakian ancestry, a thin exoskeleton made his leather neck look even thicker. He was a specimen of a Marine.

I could take him. But it wouldn't be bloody easy.

"Well, take care that his leash doesn't crush your throat, Commander. His only loyalty is to the dead. You'd do well to remember that."

The Gunnery Sergeant turned and bolted without another word. As I pondered what he'd said, I heard another voice behind me.

"Ah, getting acquainted with the crew already, Commander? Gunny Tropa's not the easiest being to make pals. An excellent showing of initiative. I expect that of my officers."

Gevin Toll stopped beside me with a wicked grin on his face, an expression that quickly changed to alarm as he was engulfed in a fast-moving hug.

It was wonderful to see him. I was grateful beyond measure.

"Thank you."

In another life I might have wept.

Finally, as all eyes stared askance at our glaring breach of protocol, I let him go so we could sit down. I couldn't stop smiling as I studied his face.

"I wired the admiral the second I found you." Gevin grinned. "I was at Starbow with Nalwist and his crew. The techs there were talking about your record."

I grinned. "Ah, you know me, I like to leave a bit of excellence wherever I go."

Gevin smiled. "Let's hope that streak continues."

"I don't know," I lifted an eyebrow. "It sounds like you've thrown me one hell of a curve."

Gevin's expression grew sullen. "I know and I'm sorry. I don't think it's impossible, though, or I wouldn't have involved you. Lieutenant Olankampf was a carrier pilot not a fighter jockey. We need a dogfighter to maneuver around this soup. Who better than the Dragon Queen?"

"Dragon Queen," I scoffed. "That little moniker was like a nail in my coffin during my trial."

"I'm sorry. I didn't mean to offend."

"It's fine," I reached across the table and patted his hand. "The Dragon Queen died of boredom in a polymer pod about ten years ago. It's just me now."

Gevin nodded solemnly. He had matured in my absence. The baby-faced lieutenant was gone, replaced by a tall, blonde, square-jawed man, and an attractive one. All that remained of the boy I knew was the clear serenity in his sea-green eyes.

"So, anyhow, ship's Captain Toll, eh? I am impressed. I never figured you for a career man. How are you?"

Gevin blushed. "I am well. Busy. Keeping this boat standing tall is a thirty hour a day job."

"I can imagine. This tug of yours is unreal. I don't know how the department heads keep up with this mob."

Something registered on Gevin's face for the briefest of moments. "Let's just say we're still adjusting to the full crew. There have been obstacles."

"I'd be surprised if there wasn't. You remember how it was after they commissioned the *Vladivostok?*"

Gevin rolled his eyes, laughing, "Oh my word, that rookie flight crew fresh from Ganivet? 'You're working on Generation Ten Jump Bomber's ladies, not garbage scows. Let's try to exercise a little finesse.' How angry were you that day?"

"If they'd have screwed up one more fuel mix, I'd have spaced them, every damned one of them."

"Well, imagine that times a hundred." Gevin smirked. "We've taken on five newly assembled flight wings in the past three months. My crew chiefs are about ready to space themselves."

My laughter turned a few heads as I reached across the table to pat Gevin on the arm. It was stirring to interact with a real friend after all this time.

I was elated.

"Man, I'd give anything to have my old Jumper back. That Gen Ten I had back then, man, I could surf without even having to think about it. The A.I. in that ship was a part of me."

"I could use you." Gevin paused for a nibble of bread. "These last couple of Flight Leaders that shipped over are a bit sketchy."

"Green?"

Gevin nodded. "Like copper gas. I have one that isn't even thirty, yet. She should still be flying supply frigates, not leading an NMK squad."

"Is the war going that badly?"

Gevin paused. I knew the expression. He was about to put a good spin on bad news.

"I don't know how much I should tell you, Nena, honestly. A lot has happened since you've been gone."

"Well, just give me the highlights. We don't get any information on Eradani other than the Freedom broadcasts and they're censored."

Gevin nodded, distracted by a mouthful of grub. "Seriously, Nena, I wouldn't worry about it right now. You have a mission to fly. Focus on that."

"That's exactly why I want to know now. The odds of me pulling this off aren't good. I'd at least like to know what the hell is going on before I'm voided. Kirpich already told me that the war was going badly, but he wouldn't elaborate on it. I need details."

"I understand, Nena. I do. But I think it's too much to deal with right now. You need to focus on the mission."

I looked away from Gevin, out over the crowd, "There's a lot to process there, too."

"Exactly. What we are doing is unprecedented. Look, I'd be blowing stardust up your six if I told you this mission was a lock. But, if it can be done, Nalwist and his crew are your best bet."

"See, that's part of what I'm talking about. Since when does the Union recruit Etherai? That little feathered chatterbox doesn't exactly inspire confidence."

Gevin wiped his mouth politely, then slid his tray to the side of the table. "All of the species in the inner spur are part of the Union now. And Commander Nalwist happens to be a prodigy in quantum engineering, as well as a very good friend."

"I'm sorry, Gevin. I didn't realize."

"I'm surprised at you, Commander. You couldn't have spent a little time studying the Tenets while you were away?"

I smiled. "I'm from Janus, remember? I wasn't born of a vaunted Paladin like you were."

"Nena, the heathen mariner, no wonder they chose you to drop down a Well."

"I think that had more to do with my prison Magister's psycho-sexual sadism, really."

Gevin's face reddened, still embarrassed by my brashness. "Let's save that story for another time, shall we? We have more than enough to work."

I heard resignation in Gevin's voice, one he couldn't mask.

There was something big going on behind the scenes. The Gunny's words lingered. I needed answers even if they were troubling. I needed the big picture.

"How badly is the war going?"

Gevin's troubled eyes stared into mine for a long few seconds before he sighed. "The Aratani have us blockaded inside the Arm. We're partially cut off from Sector Four and routed in Sector Five. The heaviest fighting is there as we seek to regain a foothold. But, right now, they have effectively driven a wedge between us and the central systems."

My blood ran cold. I'd asked for it.

"What about the colonies?"

Gevin shook his head, "Most have been occupied or blockaded. Refugees have been flooding in on any scow that will surf. A lot of them don't survive the trip."

I shifted my gaze as I thought about Janus. I didn't have family there anymore, but I couldn't begin to wrap my head around what the people there were going through. My home was a pacifist world.

"So, we gather our resources and plan a counter-strike."

"Kirpich told you that?" Gevin's eyes flashed.

"He said that's why the fleet needed the hyper-matter."

Gevin stared at me for an excruciating few seconds. "We need a win. But we also need to be very careful about how we earn it."

"What does that mean?"

Gevin stood with his tray in his hands. His expression only added to my worry. "Just fly, Nena. Don't worry about anything else. We need all the help we can get. Now, report to the medical facility and do whatever the hell Dr. Gillomi tells you too, huh? It's time to haul it in."

A smile spilled across my face. It was a phrase I always used to end pre-flight briefings.

"You heard already?"

"Before I saw you walk by. This crown isn't for decoration, you know. Now, go get yours."

I raised a formal salute. I was fully proud to do so. I grinned as I held his gaze.

"Copy that, Captain. Getting my shit together now, sir."

Gevin grinned, patting me on the shoulder as he walked away.

The trip up to medical was another potent reminder of how big the *Shaytan* truly was. It took over a half-hour to ride up out of the belly of the ship and into the command tower. I shared a tramcar with a couple of horny ensigns heading off duty and hell bent for a rendezvous in the crew hub.

I grinned as I watched them interact. If I weren't in the car, they'd have never made it to the hub. I almost felt bad for stepping on their groove.

As I stepped off the tram, I discovered that the entire central base of the command tower was the Medical Bay. It was a fully equipped interspecies medical facility and larger than some of the ones in major Union cities. Everything on this tug was a damned marvel. I was in awe of what the Navy had accomplished.

I couldn't see it then for what it was.

I was met in the reception area by a hybrid Patient Advocate. She was a new model like Viginti but created to be a matronly Uchawi female, Jizet.

I was painfully aware of my prejudice towards hybrids. They were forbidden on Janus as anathema to the Janusian philosophy of genomic exceptionalism. Mechanical enhancement was the closest thing we had to an orthodox "sin." That's why Tech Corp staff gave me the willies, too.

I'd worked very hard over the decades to get past my outmoded thinking, but ingrained patterns were hard to break. But now, from what I learned from Viginti, I found myself sympathetic.

"Commander Videt, if you'll follow me, I will take you up to Dr, Gillomi's lab."

"Thank you." I glanced around the space as I followed her to the lift. "Man, everything on this tug is just unreal. How many beds are in this place?"

Jizet smiled at my inquiry. "We have the capacity for two thousand at the main facility and five hundred more at the triage facility fore of the main hanger."

"Twenty-five hundred? By the Tenets! Are they expecting a bloodbath?"

Jizet's face slackened. Uchawi had very expressive faces. I'd never seen one go blank. It was disconcerting.

"The expectations of the command staff are beyond my purview, Commander. But we have been trained to operate at capacity as standard procedure."

The statement echoed in my brain as the lift doors closed. I was starting to get a line on what the Admiral was up to. This was an invasion ship. They were gearing up to sack Aratan.

If that was the case, a bloodbath is exactly what was going to happen.

I wasn't particularly crazy about hanging around for it, either.

Jizet showed me to the lab where Lam and Taito were setting up the alignment equipment. I guess the doctor hadn't arrived yet.

"Sorry they made you drag all this stuff up here, boys. I didn't know my brain had gone to mush."

Lam looked up from assembling the gear. "It's fine, Commander. We don't mind. It's our first time up here. We haven't been above the mess hall since we were posted."

"Damn, Nalwist keeping you on a short leash?"

Taito's brow furrowed. "The Admiral's the one holding the leash. Nalwist just has a longer lead."

Lam nodded. "Nalwist is a brilliant being. But he's no leader."

I started to reply when the door flew open. A human woman near my age swept into the room followed closely by a gaggle of residents with data pads and dilated pupils. It looked like they needed stims just to keep up with her.

"Commander, I'm Dr. Gillomi. The Admiral advises me that your encephalink is on the fritz?"

I smiled. The sarcasm was strong with this one.

"Yes ma'am. I'm afraid so. The last thing you wanted to deal with today."

The doctor grinned. She seemed amiable enough. I couldn't see why Nalwist was intimidated by her.

"Not at all. I try to stay open to where the day takes me. And there's not much going on now, so I told the Admiral I'd do it myself." Her smile was warm.

"I appreciate it. That makes me feel a lot better. The last time I got patched up I had a frightened rookie corpsman with his mother's milk still on his breath. You don't want to see the scars."

"I can only imagine." The doctor shivered. "Well, the parameters of this case are interesting. There's been some debate in the scientific community about the long-term viability of the links. Which, in your case, has been inactive for a while?"

"Yes ma'am. Right around a decade."

"A decade? Really?"

I glanced at Lam and winked. "Let's just say I was decommissioned for a good stretch. The admiral coaxed me out of retirement because he needed a pilot that wasn't in nappies."

Dr. Gillomi grinned. "I can see that. The squad meetings around here look like kindergarten classes. Most of the experienced Mariners are on the line."

"Or gone beyond." Lam bowed his head beside me.

I saw a quick flash in the doctor's eyes. She had lost someone close.

Everyone had lost someone close.

Dr. Gillomi smiled, quick to recover. "Okay so here's what we're going to do. We're going to do a holo-scan of your brain and check out the whole system. Then, if that all looks good, we will concentrate on the link connections. If there is damage, we will have to inject a new nanite system to repair and bolster the old one. That will put you out of commission for about a standard day."

"Let's hope it doesn't come to that. I don't think the Admiral will sit still for a day's delay."

The doctor smirked. "He'll wait, or he can send one of his kindergarteners."

I smiled. I genuinely liked this woman. "I'm ready when you are."

The doctor smiled back. "Let's get you healthy. Your mission's not going anywhere."

Chapter 4

After several hours of poking, prodding, probing, scanning, whining, opining, and realigning, I arrived at the Admiral's quarters in time for dinner, albeit in a funky red neck brace to keep my new nexus of nanites from running amok.

My old link had to be scrapped. I wasn't crazy about it. But it made Lam and Taito's whole damn week. They asked my permission to install a new nexus configuration they'd developed. The doctor agreed after they proved it met regs.

I balked at the idea until they told me it was one of a kind and paired with a next generation A.I. I'd be able to fly anything in the fleet without having to qualify.

It was worth the risk in case I needed to bounce.

"Commander, please come inside, I wasn't sure you'd make it." Kirpich smiled as he showed me in. "I'm glad you did."

The Admiral's quarters weren't as luxurious as I imagined them to be. It was only slightly larger than a standard officer's digs with the addition of an office and kitchenette. It was smart and minimally decorated. It said a lot about the Admiral's commitment to duty.

"Thank you, sir. I was afraid you'd be a bit salty with me gumming up your schedule."

Kirpich grinned. "I was, at first. But after I listened to Gillomi's report, I'm glad we took the precaution. That prison did a number on you."

I felt honored to have him take interest. But the gunny's words echoed.

"It did. A lot more than I realized." I looked up into Kirpich's eyes. "I thought I was holding up pretty well."

"You've held up amazingly. Most would break going through what you have. There's fire flowing in those Janusian veins."

I shot him my best sideways grin. "From go."

I saw the fire rise in his eyes just then. I'd been by myself for way too damn long to miss that. It freaked me out. Not that the Admiral was a bad looking man. But if I got laid right now, I'd be a mess.

"Wasn't Gevin supposed to be here?

Kirpich's grin was slim. He was a gentleman to not press the issue.

"He'll be along shortly. He's meeting with fleet intelligence. There's a situation developing in the Tek-hal system."

"Tehkal? There's nothing of value there."

"No. That's why the Aratani decided to build a forward munition depot there."

"By the Ancients. That's way too close to the central systems. How the hell are they sneaking into Tek-hal?"

The Admiral raised an eyebrow. He was taken with my fire.

"I'd wager it was part of their strategy all along. They kept us engaged in sectors four and five while they did an end around. We can only hope we've disrupted their advance."

"Yeah, but you don't know what could be lurking out there at the Galaxy's edge."

The Admiral nodded thoughtfully. "You're right. But the fleet is stretched too thin to send a task force to investigate. The Board of Directors is considering deploying the Home Guard."

That was heavy. That was the final stand.

I dropped my head in disbelief. I almost wished I were blissfully ignorant back in my cell. At least until the Aratani blew up the Pier.

Then I got angry. I finally get back into the world only to discover that it's gone to shit. If it wasn't for bad luck, man. Damn.

"So, what's the play? It's not hard to tell that this is an invasion ship. The proportions and dimensions still warp my newly hotwired brain. But still, invading Aratan will be a bloodbath."

Kirpich sat down on the sofa offering me the chair opposite. I couldn't wait to hear what he had to say.

"I didn't want to drop this on you your first day back. It's way too much to digest. But I think you can handle it. I need you to."

I stared him dead in the eye and nodded. The fire was gone now. It'd been replaced by fear.

"We're not invading Aratan. We're destroying it. Then, we're cleaning up their mess on the way back through."

I'd never experienced the sensation of my heart leaping into my throat until that exact moment. Then, it jumped high enough to chew on.

"Genocide?"

Kirpich scoffed. "It's not genocide. But it's a serious bloody setback for the bastards, to be sure. They'll have plenty of territory to reestablish themselves after they're disarmed."

"That's a pretty tall order."

"It is. Estimates are well over a decade. You can't clean up thirty years of chaos overnight."

"No," I bowed my head in deference for all I'd seen. "I suppose not."

Kirpich sighed as he rose from the chair. Age and responsibility weighed heavily at that moment. "Well, at least then it will be somebody else's mess. If I manage to survive the next few months, I'm going back to Proxima and drinking myself into a stupor. Then, I'm getting my boat out of drydock and going sailing."

"That sounds nice. I've never been to Proxima."

Kirpich smiled. "It's beautiful. The eastern sea makes up forty percent of its oceans. It's vast. There are islands along the equator that are breathtaking. Volcanic peaks that rise into the stratosphere. Geyser's rain warm water down from the peaks to wash across the soft obsidian sand. Even if I do die in all this, I'm still going back there. That's home."

"That sounds amazing." I smiled, imagining it. "If we do manage to escape with our skins I'll have to visit."

Kirpich winked. "Bring liquor." He eased back down onto the arm of the couch. He seemed restless. I hoped I wasn't the cause.

"So, tell me about yourself, Commander. Something that's not in your dossier. What was it like growing up on Janus?"

I grinned, leaning back into my chair. "Actually, I grew up all over the place. My father was a stalwart of Union politics since before I was born. Wherever there was a crisis or a photo opportunity that's where you'd find him."

"Wow, that's biting." Kirpich shifted in his chair. "Did you not get along?"

"It was hard for him after my mother died. He had only been ambassador a few months when she got sick. He brought us back to Janus for her convalescence. We had a wonderful villa just upriver from Bacha City. In the fall, we could sit in our garden and watch the fireworks over the city on Founder's Day. My mother loved to watch them. That's my fondest memory of her. The smile on her face as she sat among the magenta lilies on a blanket smiling as she stared up into the sky."

"That's beautiful." Kirpich smiled warmly. "What are magenta lilies?"

"They're a flower whose blooms luminesce a vivid magenta. They are gorgeous. And they smell amazing. On a muggy fall night, you could smell them all through the house. That scent always reminds me of home."

I glanced at Kirpich as I shifted in my chair. His smile was warm. He was fully engaged.

"How old were you then?"

"I'd just turned twelve. That was our last year together."

Kirpich rested his hand on my forearm. It helped.

"I will be forever grateful that I was old enough to fully appreciate her for the person she was. I cherished her every breath. When she passed, man, I was also fully cognizant of everything I'd lost, how much my world was going to change. As a result, I went a bit wild."

Kirpich's smile beamed. "Yeah? I can't see it."

I giggled, "Right? I've hidden it so well. Anyway, my father's career came first. After mom died, he buried himself in his work. I knew he loved me, but I also knew I was way down on his list of priorities. I was left to nannies and tutors and maids, and I was a wicked burden on all of them. I know now I was just trying to get his attention. But back then, I was bent on being an embarrassment to the vaunted Ambassador."

"How'd that work out?" Kirpich asked.

I grinned. "Nobody gave a shit, except for the stuffed shirts on Dad's staff. They spent a ton of coin covering up my escapades. By the time I started tertiary school though, I calmed down some. I started training and made the school G-ball team. Then, on a trip around the world to play in a tournament I got to sit in the cockpit as they made the suborbital hop. Before that bus touched down, I knew I wanted to be a pilot. After that, everything I did was aimed towards achieving that goal."

"Your dossier is a testament to your success, Commander. There are few pilots I know that match your achievements. If not for the incident with Captain Cray you could full well have been sitting here with these stars on your uniform."

Before I could reply, the door sensor chimed.

"Ah, Gevin, finally." Kirpich made for the door. "I'm ready to hit this bottle of wine."

I rose as Gevin entered the room.

"If you salute me, Videt, I'll put you swabbing bulkheads."

Kirpich chuckled as he left for the kitchen.

I raised an eyebrow. "Bad day at the office, dear?"

Gevin collapsed onto the couch and laid his head back. "It hasn't been the best, by a damn site. How are you?"

"On the mend. I spent the afternoon being over-hauled by Dr. Gillomi. She's a good doctor, thorough. I liked her. But I feel like I've had my ass kicked."

"I can imagine." Gevin's sympathetic expression made me smile. "You look pale. What's the deal with the neck brace?"

"My link had to be scrapped. It deteriorated from lack of use. So now I've been upgraded. Nalwist's mad scientists uploaded a new nexus. I have to wear the neck brace until it has time to dig in."

Kirpich returned with wine and glasses. He sat down on the couch beside Gevin. "Anything new in the briefing?"

Gevin glanced over at me.

"Don't worry about her." Kirpich winked. "She's been read in."

Gevin's eyes rounded, "Fully?"

Kirpich shrugged. "There wasn't any point in keeping it from her. She had a good bead on what's going on just by walking around the ship."

Gevin grinned. "She is exceptionally bright."

I grinned, enjoying the attention. "She's in the room, too, you know."

"We had the best conversation while we were waiting on you." Kirpich glanced at me and winked. "We were starting to hope you'd bailed."

Gevin laughed. "Not until I get a blast of this Ajian wine."

"Yes!" Kirpich did a little happy dance. "Let's get hooked up."

As Kirpich worked to uncork the bottle, Gevin shot me that exasperated look he used when I'd skirt regs. I grinned when I saw it.

"So, you're okay with this?"

"With what? The wine? You're right, I probably shouldn't. I haven't had a drink in a very long time."

Gevin glowered or tried to.

"Oh, you mean the mission? Gevin, I don't know what to think. I don't think I've wrapped my head around it, yet. It's a lot to process."

Gevin shook his head. "I don't agree with it."

"And your protest has been noted and processed." Kirpich frowned. "But I doubt the Advocates will call you any time soon. We need this to end."

I studied Gevin's face. I wasn't surprised by his reaction. He was diligent in his adherence to the Tenets. He had been raised in a monastery, after all.

"Absolutely we do. The effects of this war have spread far beyond the Union. Every species in the quadrant has been affected in one way or the other. The Aratani are vicious. They have no mercy. Destroying their planet is only going to motivate them. Sure, we'll knock down the numbers but I'm afraid it will be a war without end. In a twisted way, actual genocide would be preferable. They will fight to the last being. I have no doubt."

Gevin had a valid point. The Aratani were brutal. They'll kill one of their own if it takes out two of their enemy. They were fanatical and completely amoral. I couldn't understand how they ever achieved a technologically advanced society as irrational and belligerent as they were. Union brass had pondered for years whether there was another species leading them, but none had ever been observed.

"So, you're for taking out the star instead of the planet?"

"No." Gevin glared. "That's not what I said."

"I think it will break them." Kirpich stood to pace the room. "And if they do have some kind of hive mind leading them, it will take them out of the equation. We don't have to kill them all. We just need to let them know we can."

"In an unfair Universe, Gevin, I think that's the best we can ask for." I shook my head contemplating it. "What the hell do you think would happen if they invaded Tabak or Dhoruba? Could you see Aratani landing craft coming in over Kohav M'kdesh? We're there. Tekhal is in home space. If something is to be done, it's now."

Gevin nodded, then got a weird look on his face. He glanced over at Kirpich. "You told her about Tekhal, too?"

Kirpich nodded. "I did. Everyone else on the command staff will know after the morning briefing. She just happened to be here."

Gevin nodded. "Yeah, you're right. I already contacted Commander Lund about the stand-bye. I told him to start formulating contingencies."

"I'll have some ideas too after I read through the briefing."

Gevin's brow furrowed. "You have your own mission to prepare for. Commander Lund can handle this. He's a Mariner. You'll like him."

The phrase was a naval tradition to express one's highest esteem.

I grinned. "What makes you happy tickles me to death, love."

"Great." Gevin rubbed his hands together. "Now, when does this beast come out of the kiln, Admiral? I'm ready to grub."

Kirpich raised his glass and waited for us to follow suite. "For all those brave souls that have gone along beyond and left the rest us to do all the damned dirty work."

"Huzzah."

Chapter 5

My dinner with Gevin and Admiral Kirpich was a microcosm of fun tucked inside macrocosm of horror. In a strange way, it put me at ease. I woke up feeling better than I had in years. I was well rested and moving forth with a purpose. It's amazing how just having something meaningful to do can bolster one's joy for the day. Even when the odds were long.

I arrived at the Engineering Lab at 0600 ready to work. The hybrid mechanics were all busy with their various tasks, but I didn't see a Tech among them. I figured Nalwist would be down here already micromanaging.

"Can I help you, Commander?"

A newer hybrid, a male Simjaniian, dropped out of the bay doors of a drone torpedo ship. As soon as I saw him, I had a line on what was going on. At this stage of the war sentient beings were at a premium. These next level hybrids served to bridge the gap.

It was a solid strategy. But rife with injustice and potentially dangerous.

"I'm reporting for duty. Is Commander Nalwist here?"

The Simjaniian grinned. “Commander Nalwist is never in this early, ma’am. Lieutenants Lam and Taito are probably already up in the office, though, if you’d like to go up.”

“Thank you. What’s your name crewman?”

“Ashron, ma’am. I supervise the graveyard shift.”

“I appreciate it, Ashron. Keep up the good work.”

A big grin emerged on his face. “Thank you, ma’am.”

Be the joy you want to see I say, or some such shit. I felt for their plight. But there were way fatter fish to fry. Only victory could birth justice.

Lam and Taito were both sitting at the table in the conference room with steaming mugs and food. I held my hand up for them to stay put as I entered.

“Good morning, gentleman.”

“Good morning, Commander.”

Lieutenant Lam stood anyway offering me the seat beside him. I smiled, dropping down next to him.

“How are you feeling this morning, Commander?”

"I feel like a new woman. Thanks for asking. Dr. Gillomi is amazing. Twelve more hours in this damn neck brace and we'll be ready to get to work."

"So, what do you want to do today?" Lam asked.

"Well, I was thinking I'd run through the operations course. The doctor doesn't want me to do anything stressful, so I figured I'd kick back and watch vids. I'd like to go through the data from Olankampf's ship too."

Lam nodded. "Done and done, ma'am. No problem. We'll set you up in here so you can be comfortable. Our presentation is pretty thorough but if you have any questions page us. Taito and I have a big job today."

They radiated excitement.

"What are you two maniacs up to?"

Taito smiled. "We're going to install an A.I unit into a Berserker."

"Really? Now that is interesting."

Berserkers were a nasty bit of ordinance dreamed up by the Tabak way before they joined the Union. Traditionally, they were a mass driven load of static nano-Lawrencium housing several thousand micro-spy drones. The destruction caused by the mass driver masked the infiltration of the drones. The Union Navy wouldn't deploy them until the war with the Aratani, and now they were upgrading them.

It whispered desperation.

"So, what's the A.I. going to do?"

"The plan is to place little bombs inside the big bomb."

Taito stopped packing his tool drone and smiled. "Instead of bothering with spybots we're loading several dozen tactical nukes attached to eye drones. The A.I. gathers intelligence, determines the best targets, then guides the drones to them."

"That's nasty."

Lam nodded. "It is. But our back's against the wall. We can't afford to ignore any potential advantage."

His response troubled me. Victory at any cost was not victory. But survival was often an ugly endeavor. I feared we'd reached a point where our concept of normalcy had gone.

"That's the pervading wisdom." I said, chewing on my lip.

Lam nodded, sipping his tea. “We will prevail only as long as we do not lose sight of where we left the path. But we must survive in order to evolve.”

I nodded, impressed with his insight.

“It seems not everyone is onboard with that, though.”

Lam nodded, glancing over at Taito. “There’s been a lot of debate. Much of it stems from the vague nature of the Admiral’s mission. Everyone has pieces but no one has the whole picture, except for maybe Captain Toll. We’re set to invade something. If it’s Aratan and we don’t know until it happens? This crew will tear itself apart.”

“It’s barely holding together now.” Taito finished loading his drone and sent it on ahead.

“How so?” I asked.

“Crewing this ship has been a nightmare, ma’am. And all of it hasn’t exactly been above board. When we left Ganivet we had a crew of a hundred, barely enough to operate the ship. Since then, we’ve been picking up the survivors from various campaigns and putting them to work. There’s not a flight on this ship that was left organized to Wing level. They’re all a mish mash of orphan companies and squadrons. Commander Lund has had a hell of a time organizing them into a cohesive wing.”

I understood Gevin's frustration better. They've had to build this force from the remnants of dead vessels and decimated MCU's. The Admiral was betting on the rage of the disenfranchised to sharpen the tip of the spear.

"After so much death and despair, the rank and file have been left questioning everything. Our duty, honor and sacrifice hasn't produced the victory we were assured." Lam shook his head slowly. "The vacuum of information on the ship right now isn't working to command's advantage."

I nodded, taking it all in. I wondered if I should even try taking it up with Gevin. I had no doubt he already knew.

"So where do you stand?" I asked.

Lam shrugged. "Personally, I hope they use this load of hyper-matter to blow their whole damn star system to atoms. That's the rumor I like best. And, if I had my way, I'd give them a couple of years to regroup and then blow that place to hell, too. If any survive, they'll always be a threat."

Taito nodded thoughtfully, pointing at Lam.

"Ditto."

The duo left to go work on their Berserker leaving me with their records on the dropship. It was a technological marvel. As I read through their notes, I saw the genius in the way they reimagined hyperspace maneuvering.

Moving through hyperspace from point to point in the galaxy was a lot like surfing on an ocean. You placed yourself at the crest of a wave and rode it to your destination. In civilized space, it was an automated trip as the A.I.'s flew predetermined routes.

Dropping through hyperspace into the Equispance was more akin to diving to the bottom of the ocean. There were problems of current and pressure changes incurred for every kilometer of descent.

In other words, there was no clear path. One had to fight over, around and through the plasma currents in order to descend.

Lam and Taito took Mariner technology a quantum leap by creating plasma sails that could attract or repel hyperspace quanta. They worked as rudder, propulsion, and shield. It was next level of thinking.

I was impressed with both men, and Nalwist as well. This was an ingenious system. I couldn't wait to fly it. It would be an interesting challenge.

As I sat studying the schematics, I got the squishy feeling in my gut that the ship was coming out of hyperspace. In a sliver of a moment the ship dropped starboard in a sharp maneuver for a ship this size.

Something was up.

As I jumped from my chair to investigate, the ship shot back into hyperspace. We were most likely on our way to Tekhal.

I knew I shouldn't, but I decided to stretch my legs and drop down to the main hanger for a quick peek around.

I wanted to see Commander Lund in action.

Gevin sounded general quarters as the ship made its new course. I joined the surge to the flight deck and helped drag fuel line as the crews organized. The section I found myself in housed MKV heavy bombers. They were huge craft with a three-man crew. They could drop a thousand tons of ordinance inside the boundaries of an ordinary city. And then, no more city.

It told me we had dirtside targets. It was a start.

As the crew got up to speed, I moved up the line toward the Flight office.

I got my first look at the Generation XII Jump Bombers as I made my way aft. They were mad, mad killing machines. I had the quick urge to take one for a ride. I had qualified in every series from generation five to ten and now I was two generations behind.

It wouldn't take me too long to catch up, though, if needed.

I made my way to the command tower as I helped run ordinance to a wave of drone gunships. Their limited A.I. was purposely psychotic and programmed for a one-way trip. They were a nasty bit of chaff. Attested to by the forty kilo boxes of thirty-eight-millimeter rounds I was hustling.

Commander Lund stepped out onto the balcony of the command tower as I handed off the last box to a shaky ensign who looked terribly hungover. That kid was at the start of a very bad day.

"Commander Videt?"

"Yes, sir. Answering the call. Is there something you need me to do?"

"Yeah, get the hell up here. I don't need you injuring yourself again."

I grinned, realizing he'd been briefed by Gevin. He had warned Lund that I'd be around to stick my big nose in sooner or later.

I made my way out onto the balcony to see the entire length of the hanger splayed out before me. It was enervating. This scow was armed to the teeth.

I found Lund had moved around the curve of the balcony to check on the Marines loading into drop rings.

We were going dirtside.

"Commander Videt, reporting for duty."

Lund was a tall, distinguished looking being with sharp, dashing features. Most Liwanian males projected a refined heir, Lund carried it naturally.

"It's nice to meet you, Commander. Captain Toll speaks very highly of you."

"Thank you, sir. He did of you as well. He told you I'd be along, didn't he?"

Lund smiled. "He did, even before the alert. I'd say you bolted the second we dropped out of hyperspace."

I smiled, taken by his easy nature. "I did not. I waited until the low wing roll."

Lund grinned. "That did it for me."

"So, what would you like me to do?"

"The captain threatened grave injury if I let any harm come to you. So, how about you be my flight liaison for Jump bomber groups one and two?"

I wasn't going to complain about a desk job, but I'd rather been out in the mix.

"Roger that, Commander. Just point me to my screens."

"Don't worry, we have plenty of time. We have another hour in hyperspace. Kirpich is going to brief us before we drop out."

"The situation sounds pretty fluid."

Lund nodded. "I thought the same. The captain didn't have a lot of details, but he was told it was a black op gone bad. The Zari had taken the task."

"The Zari? Really? That's pretty ballsy even for them."

"They've really been putting it to the enemy as of late." Lund turned, keeping an eye on the progress in the hanger. "They hit out of nowhere and disappear just as quickly. Their technology is voodoo compared to what we have. So, they have the brass over the barrel. They choose their own missions and don't fall under the chain of command."

"But we still have to bail them out?"

"This is a first, as far as I know." Lund shrugged. "Something serious must have screwed up for them to call for help."

"Well hopefully, we'll catch the Aratani with their knickers down."

"Hopefully it's not a trap." Lund lifted an eyebrow. "This ship can't be much of a secret now."

My blood ran cold at the thought of it. "Is that in your contingency plan?"

"It is." Lund turned to look at me. "And I emphasized the possibility. This ship is one of a kind. It's not hard to track."

"It makes sense. They risk an expedition to plant a false flag and draw us out."

"Precisely. Good, in that there's not an invasion force backing the incursion. Bad, though, if we don't spring the trap."

I looked at Lund and nodded. "You got to whip it out before you can see if anyone wants to touch it."

Lund laughed loudly. His command staff looked aghast, mortified by his reaction. "And that is where we find ourselves, Commander."

"Well, let's just take it one step at a time," I took a deep breath. "We train to act so we don't overreact. We'll just have to be on the lookout for what they don't want us to see."

Lund winked. He was of great humor. “Welcome to the flight staff, Mariner.”

My smile was genuine. “My only wish is to serve.”

Chapter 6

The flight deck was cocked, locked and ready to rock by the time Admiral Kirpich's huge holographic head appeared above the hanger deck.

From my perspective I could see it floating about every ninety meters or so along the length of the flight deck. If not for the war we'd have enough room to run about thirty gravity ball courts at once. That was only half as dangerous.

As everyone snapped to attention, I noticed a few beings around the periphery who did not.

Gunny Tropa and his squad among them.

Commander Lund noticed them as well.

"We are ten minutes from egress in the Tekhal system. A division level force of Zari is pinned down on the fifth planet by two Aratani gunships. A Zari cruiser is set to rendezvous with us at the system's perimeter and will escort the first wave to their targets. The Shaytan will not be entering the system. If you are in trouble and can jump, micro-stream courses have been relayed to your ship's computer. Get yourself out of the system and we'll pick you up.

"The Aratani have entered home space. This incursion is the first in nearly seven centuries. No matter what your politics are or how you feel about me or the situation we find ourselves in. There will be no personal victories without total victory. When we arrive on that fine day, then we can have it all out. The Union will ultimately be strengthened by this experience, our society enhanced through the guidance of those of us who fought to see the war through. But we must secure that future first. The universe grants no entitlements. If we are to continue, we must move now as one."

I saw the frustration in Kirpich's eyes. "Give them hell out there, folks. I'll see you on the other side."

He was a good man in an impossible situation. My heart went out to him.

"Alright, Commander, if you follow A'sharim, she'll get you hooked up with a console. Your jump bombers are going in wave two."

I raised an eyebrow. "Second wave?"

"The Admiral is going to soften them up with artillery first."

"From where?"

"From the two destroyers deploying from the aft dock."

I raised both eyebrows, "We have an aft dock?"

Lund smiled. "We do. It's home to two new destroyers' custom built for the *Shaytan.* You'll see them once the array is established. Now get to your station."

"Copy that. I'll keep my eyes open."

A' sharim led me inside the tower and up a level to the Combat Center. We had to push our way through the rushing hordes of analysts and techs preparing for launch. I followed her to a workstation in the back corner.

"I figured I'd get you out of the fray, Commander. It gets hectic in here."

"So, I noticed. It's been a good long while since I sat in on a mission from Ops."

A'sharim grinned. She was created to look like an Earther like Viginti. There were striking similarities between the two. It was apparent they were patterned on a standard genetic template. I couldn't help but wonder if there were some Janusian geneticists involved in their creation. They were flawless.

"Things haven't changed much. You'll have all the gun camera and telemetry info on six screens. If there's anything you want to focus on, they can be merged into one or two screens by pulling the others to the screen you want to enhance. You can also call up the array and follow your squad in real time. Sometimes that's easier to focus on when targets have been engaged."

"It can be a lot to process." I said.

"Definitely. Also, if there's anything you want to mark in the recording just click in and out on the timestamp. It will be marked across the network and analyzed post-op."

"Thank you, A'sharim. It'll take a second or two, but I'll get back in the swing."

"You're welcome, ma'am. I'm sure you will." As she walked away, I got the feeling she wasn't convinced.

It took me a fast five seconds to get my network up and running. I almost called her back to brag.

As I sat gloating, I felt the ship drop out of hyperspace.

The ship was rocked immediately from something explosive landing against the shields.

As the array came up, we saw the Zari cruiser already under attack by an Aratani Marauder.

Lund's voice rang through all the speakers on the flight deck. "Change of plans. I want gun-drones and NMK squads one through four out on my mark."

Time for me to go to work.

The ship rocked again as the jump bombers rose from the deck. As soon as the flight boss hit the green light, they were gone.

I missed being strapped into one.

I pulled all my ships up on the screens keeping the gun cameras on two screens while I opened the other four on the ship's camera array. The Zari cruiser was taking a hell of a beating from the Marauder.

Marauders were a sick bit of technology. They were mid-sized cruisers with a crew of about three hundred. The ships rested on a massive power plant that powered their vicious forward batteries. They were nearly impossible to catch in real space. And pure hell to deal with when they stopped.

My flight leader, a Lieutenant Artine, did the smart thing and led the bombers down and aft of the Marauder. They scrambled out behind the ship and looped around to hit it from stern to bow. Then, in a bold move, the squad split. Half went after the bridge while the others dropped below to take out the shield on the power plant.

Their first pass rocked that scow.

As they made their way around for another pass, the gun-drones tore into the forward batteries. They were small enough to slip inside the shields and unleash hell. Within seconds one of the forward guns was down.

The marauder responded by trying to close the gap between them and the Zari cruiser. As the jump bombers unleashed another volley, one of the destroyers rushed in putting themselves between the marauder and the cruiser.

The new destroyer was a Union gunship on steroids. It matched the marauder well.

The marauder unleashed another volley from its remaining guns. In the glow I noticed its port side shields waver. The jump bombers had taken a toll.

I keyed the microphone to speak to the group leader. "Lt. Artine, this is CIC, registering shield damage, port side. See if you can get that nasty bitch to yaw starboard."

The lieutenant chuckled as he keyed in. "Copy that, CIC."

I paged A'sharim. It only took a second for her to respond. "Yes, Lieutenant?"

"Reporting shield damage on the marauder, port site. Directing NMK to force it starboard and set it up for the destroyer."

"Confirming shield damage. Passing it up to Lund."

The destroyer's shield held as it opened fire on the marauder. Its firepower was impressive. The marauder knew it was in trouble and fired its maneuvering thrusters to turn starboard and protect its bad side.

The jump bombers were caught inside the turn as they fired on the port side shield. Two of my camera screens went blank as their ships succumbed to the marauder's lunge. The blast from the remaining ships took the shield out completely.

Lund recalled the jump bombers as the marauder set course to run. As soon as the bombers cleared the area, the destroyer and Zari cruiser unleashed hell on the marauder.

With its shields down, the marauder didn't make it a hundred kilometers before it exploded. As it devolved into a navigation hazard, the cruiser and destroyer jumped to the inner system.

Before I had time to process our success, A'sharim keyed in. "Commander Lund would like a word with you."

I frowned as I powered down my screens.

What the hell did I do now?

Commander Lund was on the balcony rearranging his launch priorities with the flight boss. I hung back out of earshot while they conferred. As I waited, a whole flight of torpedo drones headed for the launch tunnel.

I got the feeling that our fluid situation was deepening.

“Commander, that was a good catch on the shields.” Lund smiled as I approached.

“Thank you, Commander. I’m glad to finally be of use. Are we prepping to relaunch?”

“For stand-by. We have a better understanding of what’s happening on the ground now so we’re redeploying. I have a different task for you.”

“What do you need me to do?”

“I want you to go up to Ops and see if you can figure out where this Aratani carrier is.”

As we spoke, I noticed the launches had stopped. The bay doors were closing as well.

“We’re jumping?”

“Affirmative.” Lund nodded. “We’re not alone out here. Aratani marauders weren’t built for long range deployment. They hitched a ride out here. Captain Toll is going to jump the perimeter of the system and launch sorties. We’re trying to make them believe a task force has arrived and see if we can flush them out. I need you to figure out where they are in case they don’t take the bait.”

“Copy that,” I saluted the Commander. He was a worthy officer. “I’m on my way.”

I shagged ass to a turbo lift and split for Ops. I hadn’t been to the bridge yet and was excited to see the ship from up top. As I made my way up, I felt the ship drop back out of hyperspace. This time there weren’t any crazy maneuvers or explosions so Gevin must have found an empty parking spot.

Operations consumed the entire deck just below the bridge. With so many moving parts on this big beast it took a whole battalion of operators to operate it. I stood at the periphery looking for Viginti

Luckily, she saw me first. She was on top of me before I made her out.

“Commander, I have a spot for you. Lund is preparing a squad of recon probes? He said they were for you.”

Ah, brilliant idea!

"Yeah, we think there might be some wallflowers out there that are too shy to dance. I'm going to flush them out."

I grinned as Viginti attempted to process the vernacular. "We do as we must, Commander. If you'll follow me, I'll show you to your station."

It sucked not having my uplink operational. Here I could ride along inside the probes and guide them intuitively but without my link I'd have to operate them virtually. It was a definite handicap.

I settled in quickly, signaling the flight boss I was online. As soon as I did, I got a three-minute countdown clock. It activated in green below the red 'jump' clock that blinked just below ten minutes. Gevin wasn't letting his seat get warm and Lund wanted the probes out before the jump.

I found myself having to take a deep breath to get a handle on the rush I was experiencing.

I felt like I belonged again.

As I waited for launch, I clicked over to the array to get a feel for the space we were occupying. We were way out-system, just inside heliopause. There was plenty of icy junk floating around big enough to hide a carrier. I started surveying potential targets as the clock wound down. If they were here, I'd find them.

I took control of the lead ship as soon as it cleared the launch tunnel. The probes were bound together for launch and as I did a few quick maneuvers to get a feel for it, the whole squadron moved in lockstep.

These new probes were dynamic. Without my link though, I'd have to rely on their onboard systems to carry out their assignments while I piloted the leader.

I quickly assigned an ice ball to each ship and sent them out as I set course for a rogue planetoid about eighty-thousand kilometers away. The Union database had it cataloged as Mahaja, the name of an ancient Tabakian Queen. She must have been one frosty bitch to inspire the cartographers to name this stone after her.

I set course for an extremely low pass around the planetoid, only a few thousand meters. I would still get picked up by scanners, but it wouldn't be until I was right on top of them. As I pushed the probe at top speed around the planetoid's limb, I discovered there wasn't anything there.

As I changed course for the next ice ball on my list, a commotion erupted on the far side of the room. I couldn't hear everything being said but I got the gist. One of the new destroyers had taken heavy damage and couldn't jump out of the fray.

The Aratani carrier had taken the bait and joined the battle.

I recalled the probes before the order came through but couldn't get them back onboard before we jumped. As soon as we sliced into hyperspace, another Aratani carrier jumped on top of our last position. Two of the probes exploded against its shield.

I ordered the other probes to scramble in-system and get as much information as possible.

I keyed Viginti, who appeared at my side quickly. "There's another carrier out there. It jumped in right after we left. They know we're here. They're tracking us."

A quick flash of worry passed across her face as she pulled her mic close to inform Kirpich. It was a trap. The Aratani weren't messing around.

"What do you want me to do?"

"Keep those probes on that second carrier," Viginti ordered. "I want to know the second it jumps."

"Roger that, changing to parallel course."

The carrier launched two marauders to claim the space before it jumped. I sent the information to Viginti as I sent the probes in for a closer look.

Another commotion erupted as the destroyer succumbed to enemy fire. Four hundred more souls lost to this damn war. I hung my head as my probes harassed the marauder.

I didn't know what Kirpich and Gevin were going to do, but it was time to shit or hop off the head. I wasn't crazy about abandoning the Zari. But if the Well mission was a chance to take these fuckers out, we needed to pursue it, quickly.

I had to see it through.

I felt a heavy shimmer in my gut as we came out of hyperspace. As it subsided, the ship shuddered beneath my feet and quickly again. I grimaced at Viginti flipping my screen to the array.

Gevin dropped us right in the middle of the fight.

The immediate onboard weapons response was staggering. Its rapid pulse resonated through the hollow hull of the ship in kinetic bursts. It was quite enough to set one's teeth on edge.

I had only gotten a cursory sense of it when I researched the ship. But as I watched it rain hell on the Aratani carrier I found it supremely impressive.

"Videt, Lund is dropping gun drones for you with an NMK flight on its six. We need to level the field so the Zari can bug out."

I was surprised to hear from Kirpich, more so that he'd asked me to lead a surface assault. It was my first in ages. I took another quick deep breath to try and relax.

"Copy that, sir. Countdown initiated."

And so, there I was, sitting dead in the middle of a shit storm to beat all others and I couldn't quit smiling.

Chapter 7

Tekhal Five or Upepo, was a dead rock with a tenuous atmosphere and crazy amounts of volcanic activity. I guided the gun-drones through the crossfire and down into the atmosphere using the smoke from the closet active crater to mask our approach.

Our target was a mechanized assault team attempting to retake the weapons depot the Zari captured. The compound had taken a beating from orbit but as the drone's scanners came up, I saw that the Zari had a shield in place over a good piece of low ground east of the depot.

We had to keep the Aratani away from the Zari long enough for them to get off the ground.

"Lt. Artine, are you sucking wind, yet?"

A giggle as his mic keyed up. "Transitioning now, Commander. Waiting for orders, ma'am."

Well, I'll be damned. Lund put me over the operation. He must be desperate.

"Once you level out, circle around east of my signal before you begin your attack run. The Zari set themselves up a blind out there and I want you to drive the mechs away from it."

"Copy that, Commander. I see it. We'll drive them toward the compound."

"Excellent. And if you see anything weird out there, let me know."

Artine chuckled again. "This whole bloody reality is weird, Commander. But we've got eyes up."

"Way to be, Mariner. Give 'em hell."

"Thanks, Commander. Copy that and out."

I grinned as I throttled the drones up to attack speed. I was really starting to like that kid.

I jumped the drones up out of a ridge south of the mechs and hit them full tilt. It was twisted metal and blood orange carnage as we raced across the plain. We'd caught them completely off guard.

The guns on these new drones could place a thirty-eight-millimeter round every ten-square centimeter in swath 6 meters wide and 90 meters long before you had to let the guns cool. A squadron twenty ships wide could turn a battlefield into oozy jelly in just one pass.

We put a hell of a bite on the mechs.

As they returned fire, I pulled the drones up quickly over the compound then back down on the deck to cover our escape. As soon as I was out of the way, Lieutenant Artine's squad came in hot and heavy releasing incendiary bombs across the field. The I-bombs were nasty bastards in a low-pressure atmosphere. Their charge spread like wildfire and turned the mechs that survived the initial blast into easy bake ovens.

A flame broiled Aratani was a happy one. Peaceful, too.

Our first two passes reduced the ground force by half. I had enough ammo for the drones to make another pass, but I waited to let Lt. Artine's squad take another shot with some artillery of their own. Their energy weapons packed a hell of a punch, too, but I liked it better when stuff exploded instead of just melting into slag. But I was all for whatever made the Aratani happy.

"Flight Leader, this is Zari actual. We're in the clear and powering for lift-off. Thanks for breaking us out."

"Copy that, actual. The jump bombers will escort you out. We'll cover you."

"Copy that, Leader."

"Copy that, Commander."

I keyed Artine privately. "Keep an eye on that crossfire on your way out."

"Copy that, too, ma'am. It's intense up there."

"Be safe." I smiled. "I'll see you shortly."

I brought the drones around from the east and hammered down, fanning the width of the plain to take out the stragglers. As soon as I opened fire the Zari dropped their shield and leaped skyward at an insane velocity. I wasn't sure the bombers could keep up. Those chicks were nuts.

The Zari were a fascinating phenomenon. They were an ancient cult of warrior women from a system near the Horsehead Nebula.

The Yakaran race evolved from a fierce felinoid species on the vast grasslands of Caldai's eastern continent. A trait of their species was a tertiary gender system. This trait is most common in insectoid species. The Yakarans have brood mothers and infertile "worker" women, who, across the space of millennia, grew to be the warriors and protectors of the Yakaran tribes.

After a fierce interplanetary war in which the warrior women were nearly wiped out, they started a civil war within Yakaran society. They rallied the disenfranchised workers to their cause and left Caldai for an abandoned base on the dead world of Bel Zari, the most distant planet in the Caldaiean system.

And there in the dark on that dead world they became the baddest force in the known galaxy. They answered to no one. They were beholden to no one. And they absolutely took no shit.

I was glad they were on our side.

I finished my pass and guided the drones off world. The battle above the planet was still intense. The *Shaytan* and its remaining destroyer were giving the Aratani carriers all they could handle.

Both Aratani gunships had been destroyed as well as the Zari cruiser. The Zari coming off world jumped right into the fight and were absolutely afflicting one of the carriers. The Shaytan focused its firepower on the other carrier and let the Zari have their fun.

Within minutes they had breached the reactor on the carrier and lost a few of their own in the explosion. Whatever those tiny ships packed, it was devastating. Their technology was centuries beyond Union capabilities, and they had no desire to share it.

As I turned the ships over to the A.I.'s for docking the flight boss sounded the recall order.

I pulled off my VR set and saw the jump clock counting down from five minutes. It would be a hell of a stunt to get everything squared away on the deck before we punched out. They must have thought the Aratani had reinforcements close.

I got up to go find Viginti and found Kirpich standing at the front of the room.

"Ah, Videt. Good job down in the dirt. No ships lost. You should do this for a living."

I grinned. It was reassuring that he could keep his humor in this mess.

"I used to have a job like that. It didn't pay worth a damn."

When he laughed, I couldn't help but join in. It raised a few eyebrows and caused more than a couple of scowls. "It still doesn't." He winked. "But it's the only game in town."

"Just my luck."

As we talked, I could feel the vibration from the big guns underfoot. The carrier had lost power and was listing toward Upepo. The *Shaytan* kept firing until it started dropping in pieces into the gravity well.

The battle was ours but at tremendous cost.

Kirpich nodded with satisfaction as cheers went up from the analysts surrounding us.

"Get some rest, Commander. I want you in the morning briefing at 0600 tomorrow."

I caught my tongue before asking why. It was the first time in a long time that had happened. "Yes, sir. Copy o-six hundred."

Kirpich grinned, returning my salute and my wink.

"Dismissed."

I took the long way back to my berth to get a sense of the battle. I'd get the official post op briefing in the morning, but I needed the view from the trenches. Sometimes their voice was lost in the scramble for facts.

I made my way up to the Hive to see if I could find Lt. Artine and his squad. I felt responsible for them now.

As I walked through the rec room to the barracks, I saw just how hard the battle had been.

I was surrounded by walking wounded left restless and staring into space. Their frazzled countenance born of the horror of war and left me grasping for meaning. Shrines were already being erected on empty bunks as friends gathered in clusters along the length of the room. And so, I found the lieutenant and his squad standing for the pilots they lost against the marauder.

Artine grinned, saluting as I approached. He knew who I was, instantly.

"Commander Videt. Thanks for coming up. We all wanted to meet you."

I returned their salute. They were the cutest bunch of babies I'd ever seen.

Artine was Bituin. Bituins are cunning warriors. They were a sleek, slender, amphibian race with surprisingly good cheer. It was no wonder he laughed at my bullshit. He'd be a fun audience.

"And I, you, Lieutenant. You and your whole squad. That was precision work down in the dirt."

The whole squads' eyes lit up.

"Thank you, ma'am. Those were our first missions in a while. We thought we'd be rusty."

"Where were you posted before?"

Artine looked at his squad. "We were flying cap at Altama when our carrier was ambushed. It had to be scuttled. The aftermath was a bloodbath. We had to fight like hell to get survivors out. Only three jump squadrons and a heavy bomber wing survived intact. We've been with the admiral ever since."

I found it interesting that he said, *'with the Admiral,'* not the ship or Captain Toll. The admiral had to really put himself out there to pull this crew together, even if they weren't all in his pocket.

"Well, I appreciate your help. Hopefully, the next few weeks will be quiet."

"Are we really putting together a weapon to take out Aratan?"

This came from a Tabakan ensign at the back of the group. She was so young her chin spikes hadn't grown in yet. The group admonished her for speaking out of turn.

"I have no idea what the Admiral and Captain Toll have planned. I was brought in to test experimental equipment."

It was a skinny version of the truth. The group seemed to take it in stride.

"I'm sorry, Commander." Lt. Artine looked on edge. "We're all a bit stir crazy. There's not a lot of information dropping from topside."

"You don't have to tell me about stir crazy, Lieutenant. Trust me, I get it. My guess is that whatever they're planning, the situation is too fluid to settle on a course of action, yet."

"Well, that makes sense." Artine glanced around the barracks. "Whatever they're planning has to be massive. They didn't build this thing to ferry pilgrims."

I got a giggle out of that. The kid was sharp. "Exactly. So don't worry. You'll know when you know. If I were you, I'd park in the simulators and stay sharp. If you really want a challenge, take a trainer on something bigger like a troop cruiser or a repair frigate. You never know when it will come in handy."

There was a knowing, a rare flash in Artine's aquamarine eyes. He took my meaning and struggled with the idea that escape could well become his only option. Altama weighed on his mind.

"That's actually not a bad idea, Commander," the Tabakan girl chimed in. She was a bold one. "It beats sitting around here listening to all these maleoids talk shit."

I liked this one. Just wait until she'd grown all her spikes. "What's your name ensign?"

The others laughed as I moved to stand before her.

"Thala Kesek, ma'am."

"Well, Thala Kesek, ma'am. I guess you better hop on in there and learn to fly everything you can then. There'll never be an end to that. And versatile pilots will make big bank come peacetime."

"Copy that, Commander," Thala smiled. "I want to have my own merchant fleet someday."

Her exuberance was alluring. "That's a great goal, ensign. You can give me a job. I know my way around just about every scow in the fleet. That should be worth a few chips."

"And then some." Thala nodded earnestly. "I need all the help I can get."

I grinned. "I'll hold you to that. Because I have no clue what I'm going to do after this is over."

Thala chuckled. "Who are you kidding? They'll probably make you a Magister and ship you off to Ganivet to powder asses."

A Magister? I found the thought revolting. Britva Lopast's macabre presence flashed in my mind.

"Yeah, that's a hard pass on both counts. I don't know what I'll do but I'm sure as hell not reenlisting."

"That's a shame, Commander. You do exhibit some talent."

The room jumped to attention at the sound of Lund's voice.

"As you were." Lund's eyes followed the wounded as they eased back onto bunks or on to pacing. It was hard to tell if he was sympathizing or assessing them.

Hopefully, both.

I held out my hand for him to join us. "I just wanted to meet your elite jump bomber squadron, Commander. They do good work. I wish I could keep them."

Lund smiled, nodding. "They certainly shone well today. I'm sorry about Quan and Nyam."

The squad gave Lund the tribute salute. "Thank you, sir."

"I hate to break things up, but I need to steal Commander Videt away."

I wasn't sure I liked the sound of it.

Artine smiled. "Certainly, sir. We still have stuff to lock down. Commander Videt, it was a pleasure. Hopefully, we'll meet again soon."

"I look forward to it, Lieutenant."

"Thank you for the advice, ma'am." The Tabakan girl's smile was infectious.

I turned to her and winked. "The first time's free."

I followed Lund out of the barracks and into the rec room. He kept a close eye on his pilots as we made our way along. He looked relieved when we exited the complex into the passageway.

I wanted to inquire but thought better of it. Every commander interacts with his troops differently. It wasn't for me to gauge or engage.

"So, giving my new boots advice, Commander? Should I ask?"

It was an inquiry with a subtle edge.

"I just told them to stay in the simulators. Stay sharp. I told the ensign to run the trainer in a cruiser. She wants to fly merch after the war."

Lund took in the information without expression. Something was on his mind.

We walked past the lift station on the far side of the hub. Lund looked around to make sure we were alone. His need for secrecy put me ill at ease.

"We took a hell of a beating in that battle, Commander. Losing that destroyer was a real hit. We're going to have to reassess how we move forward now. Our plan for the mission is shot."

"That bad, huh?"

Lund nodded. "Yeah, that bad."

"So, what's the play? There had to be backups."

"Of course, but none nearly as palpable." Lund turned to watch a tram race by. "We have a lot of damage to the ship that needs repaired as well as the losses to the wings. It's going to be rough trying to guard the Well in the condition we're in."

"I guess that's why Kirpich wants me in the briefing in the morning."

Lund nodded. "We need to muster all of the brain power, grit and experience on this ship to get a handle on this hiccup."

I grinned, nodding my head. "I don't know about brain power, but I have grit and experience jumping for days."

Lund smiled. "Well, whatever you bring to the table, Videt, just make sure you got it on lock tomorrow morning, because we're getting eyeball deep in this."

"Copy that, Commander. Looks like I have home-work to do."

Lund nodded. He seemed doomed to the task. "It's time to haul it in."

Chapter 8

Admiral Kirpich's conference room was at fever pitch when I rolled in twenty minutes early. I thought I'd have time to watch the scene develop. Judging by the number of empty cups and stimulant filters thrown in the dustbin, some of these souls had been here for hours.

What caught my eye first was a spirited debate raging between Nalwist and someone who appeared to be the systems chief. He was an Alazai, rank Major, and all the way pissed off. He had his claw in Nalwists' face and was raising hell in three languages.

It was but one occurrence among many. The stress was showing.

I took the seat closest to the door and entertained myself until I saw Kirpich and Gevin at the door. I shot Kirpich a wink as I jumped out of my chair and saluted.

"Admiral on deck!"

I put enough lung into it to cut through the din. Nalwist looked genuinely relieved as he snapped to.

The Alazai wasn't near done with him yet.

"At ease." Kirpich made his way to the head of the table where Viginti waited with a steaming mug of something and a data jewel. Kirpich smiled slipping the jewel into a belt pouch before taking the mug. "All right, folks. We have a lot to cover. I know some of you have been on your feet double shift. So, let's get to it. Major Pava, give me good news."

The Alazai did his best to contain himself. Stress emanated in waves as he drew a deep breath. Nalwist hung his head as he sat down.

That bird was messed up.

"I hate to be the one to start off your day, Admiral, but the news isn't great. We lost two shield generators and their powerplant is offline as well. We have major hull breaches on fore gunnery decks one through four and minor damage to fore maneuvering thrusters."

Kirpich didn't look enthused, but he didn't appear angry either. "What's the estimate to get the powerplant back online?"

That's when the Major twitched. A sudden jerk across his big face.

I had a feeling Nalwist was the cause.

"Well sir, we have a few hitches with that. We're working now to get the old generators out and shore up damage. We're having supply problems because Commander Nalwist has used up most of the ship's metal supply and has yet to replace it."

Kirpich frowned. "Below catalog?"

"Below common sense, sir. The foundries haven't logged time in weeks, and I have equipment out for repair. He has half a dozen repair drones I need. I don't know what the hell he's been doing down there but he sure as hell isn't following regs."

No sugar coating there. I liked that guy.

"Commander Nalwist, an explanation?"

Nalwist rose from his chair like he was heading for the gallows. He glanced at Kirpich with a hung expression and cleared his throat to speak. "I'm doing the best I can, sir. My staff is overwhelmed. I've been pulling materials for repairs and replacing them as the job clears. I didn't want to waste elemental material for things I didn't need at the time. As I told the Major, sir, I have more than enough to facilitate repairs, but it must be processed and again at zero lost waste because we can print exactly what we need from the catalog."

Okay. Nalwist wasn't as big an idiot as I thought. His logic was sound, but he obviously wasn't familiar with the principle of naval expediency, wasting three-quarters to save half the time.

Kirpich's face was blank. I'd bet he was having the same thought. "And what is your estimate to complete the Major's list?"

"If I shut down equipment repair and put everyone on it, fifty hours."

Kirpich's neutral expression turned sour. The Major came unglued.

"Fifty hours? Are you kidding me? There's an Aratani carrier group hunting us, and you want us to what? Find a small moon and pedal around it for a few days while you get your shit together, Commander? And I told you I need my drones too. I can't get everything installed without them."

The peanut gallery started getting noisy again. Their composure was tenuous. The bad situation had just been ratcheted up by a factor of ten. They weren't responding well to it. They looked exhausted.

Kirpich held up his hand and the Major reigned himself in.

"That's enough. That's not constructive." Kirpich rubbed his eyes. "Nalwist, how many techs would it take to run repair a full four watches as well as both foundries?"

“My word, Admiral, I’d have to say at least fifty. But it would still take a while to get them up to speed.”

Kirpich drummed his fingers on the table, considering. He leaned over to Gevin and said something. Gevin’s brows arched. After a second’s reflection, he looked at Kirpich and nodded.

“Viginti, I want fifty hybrids programmed for mechanical engineering, metallurgy, and machining. How long until you can have them online?”

I saw a tiny waver in Viginti’s cheek. Her face geared quickly to a friendly smile.

“Twelve hours, sir, no less. Those trainers are extensive.”

Kirpich nodded. “Nalwist, I want those foundries up and running within the hour. Put everyone on it. Your mechanics and shift relief will be there for third watch.”

“Wenago, I want you to prioritize your list and we’ll go by the numbers. I want that powerplant up and running. I want maneuvering thrusters online, second. Artillery is a low priority.”

“And a big job, sir,” Wenago nodded emphatically.

"Okay, so we'll seal off that whole section and wait until we get to Anowi." Kirpich frowned.

As Kirpich spoke, a charge shot through me like high volt static. I looked out of the door to see the Queen Mother of the Zari with two of her guards.

I stood and bowed to give the room a heads up.

Gevin looked up as the Queen Mother entered the room. It went dead silent.

Kirpich came around the table to greet her. "Queen Mother, we're honored by your presence."

"Thank you, Admiral Kirpich. Thank you for taking us in. I came to see if I can offer my assistance."

"That's very gracious of you, Your Majesty. We're still trying to assess what we need."

I caught Kirpich's eye as he turned to escort the Queen Mother to his seat at the table.

His eyes went wide. I shook my head and shrugged.

The Queen Mother held all eyes in the room as she shirked aside her cape and sat in Kirpich's chair. She was a magnificent being. Her feline features held both the possibility of ferocity and the bliss of Zen in equal measure. Her nanite armor was skintight, an ink-black snakeskin that rippled of its own accord. The computer displays on her wrists worked in a bizarre three-dimensional array that orbited her wrists like electrons. She was a powerful woman in her prime.

She commanded the room.

"Admiral Kirpich, I invite you to bring the Shaytan to Bel Zari for repairs."

For the first time that morning I saw a spark in Kirpich's eyes. He was curious.

So was I.

So was the command staff. Tongues wagged immediately.

Kirpich held up a hand to silence the room. "I thank you, Your Highness, but that's quite a bit out of our way."

The Queen Mother held Kirpich's gaze. There was no question who the apex predator was.

"You're in no shape to fight that carrier group if they catch up." Her eyes took in everyone in the room. "The Aratani are an egregious enemy. There's no dishonor in acknowledging it. They are also a blight on the galaxy. They need to be dealt with, permanently."

The fire in Kirpich's eyes sparked anew.

The Queen Mother saw it. "I am aware of this ship's mission, Admiral. I want to make sure it succeeds."

That's when the room really got lively.

"How the hell does she know what the mission is? Most of the officers on this ship haven't gotten a straight answer about it."

This popped out of one of the combat engineers. Kirpich glanced his way, but I don't think he'd caught who'd said it.

"Queen Mother, I'm not sure what you've heard but we're weighing our options on how best to proceed. Especially now."

The Queen Mother's expression didn't change. My guess was she was evaluating Kirpich's command strategy.

I don't think she dug it.

"The objective, as I was told by Paladin Toll, is to destroy Aratan."

Gevin shot up in his chair, his face a mask of surprise. That this came from his father packed a hell of a sting. "A Paladin told you this?"

“Your father told me this, Captain. Personally, when I was last on Earth. That was the purpose of this ship from the beginning.”

The din grew louder.

“So, this is what he means by taking the fight to the enemy? Genocide?”

“It goes at the heart of the Tenets.”

Kirpich’s face reddened. He was playing a dangerous game. When the rank and file got ahold of this it would be another shit storm. We had enough to deal with already.

As he opened his mouth to speak, the Queen Mother cut him off.

“I understand your moral dilemma. Your Tenets have served you well since our first contact. We would not be in this fight now, if not. But I think what you must realize is there is no peace to be made with these creatures. Their civilization is abhorrent. And they will fight to the last being. The question becomes, who is the better galactic citizen? The answer is obvious.”

The Queen Mother turned to address the room. “The central systems are complacent, but they aren’t blind. They need the Union. More, I think, than you need them. And they don’t want a threat festering at their borders. If Aratan is destroyed it would make a statement they cannot ignore and perhaps get them to help clean up this mess and rebuild. It would be to their advantage."

The room was silent.

The civilizations in the central systems were thousands to millions of years older than any of the ones in the Union or anywhere out near the rim. Most were non-corporeal and could shift from matter to energy. A majority spent their time in intricate Metaverses where they lived random lives as entertainment.

Union physicists have long speculated that their Metaverses were real and valid. The poets have said that could very well be what we're all doing right now and in infinite layers.

To keep their worlds up and running the Ancients employed Hoplite races to keep the wheels greased. And the Union has, over the centuries, become their supplier of choice.

"What if it has the opposite effect?" Gevin asked. "What if we alarm them?"

That got the noise back on point. Tenets aside, you shouldn't piss off the customer.

Man, I was glad the Admiral let me in on this.

“That, I very much doubt.” The Queen Mother shifted in her chair. “I’ve heard stories about the Ancients. They are far from pure. Imagine the galaxy five million years ago. What they’ve done to survive cannot be fathomed. But survive they did and so must we.”

From what I could gauge the Queen Mother’s words hit home. But there was plenty of time to over analyze.

“So, I put it to you, Admiral. Divert to Bel Zari for a week. Between your staff and mine we’ll have the ship built back better than specs. There your Well pilot can prepare for her mission in a safe space.”

Kirpich’s surprise was so sudden he looked like he’d swallowed a bug.

The Queen Mother knew where all the bodies were buried.

“And we must stay within our window of opportunity with the Antithessians, Queen Mother. I can’t afford a whole week. It’s too long a trip.”

“Then we will get done what we can and take the rest along. How many troops can you berth?”

Kirpich turned to Viginti.

"A thousand if we clear the destroyer base."

Heads dropped in memory of the destroyer crew.

"A thousand and support equipment. That will work." The Queen Mother smiled.

It was menacing.

Kirpich looked at Gevin. The two studied each other for a long moment before Kirpich nodded.

I couldn't begin to unwind the intricacies of their relationship or the weight of responsibility lying on their shoulders. All I could rely on was the uncommon strength of Gevin Toll's character. I trusted him to be my guide in this.

"Excellent." The Queen mother stood, settling her cloak around her in a flourish. "I will contact my people immediately. They'll be prepared when we arrive."

Kirpich bowed as she passed. "Thank you, Queen Mother. I appreciate your help."

"Don't thank me yet, Admiral. Wait until we get out of this alive."

Chapter 9

The jump to Bel Zari was a manic affair. All hands stood for repairs.

I volunteered to pitch in, but the admiral wouldn't allow it. He assigned a Tech Corp ensign to guide me through the trainers for the dropship.

I needed it. Damn bird.

It was an ingenious system but controlling the flight variables was a nightmare, even with an AI. The only way I could make changes was to get in the simulator and feel it out, but I needed my link and medical was slammed.

Dr. Gilomi had me on her list.

The ensign was new boots fresh from Ganivet. His first assignment was to the carrier, *Nozai,* but it was destroyed on its run home. Kirpich swung through and picked up the orphans.

The ensign, Raibous, was Uchawi. Their home world, Makatifu, was twice the size of most life-bearing planets. They were a studious race. Their seat of government existed in a city of galaxy class colleges and tech schools. Their practice of government was the ward of academics.

It sounds weird but I heard it cut out the payola.

Raibous seemed an aware, kind being. He just talked a lot when he was nervous.

I made him nervous.

"So how were things on Ganivet? It's been a long time since I was there."

Raibous shrugged. "It was hectic my last few days. We lost so many ships at Alkoo that my entire class sat around the rings without a berth. The only ones that got out were the marines."

"Where were they headed?"

Raibous' placid silver eyes widened. "Sector Five."

"Right into the grinder." I bowed my head.

"I'm afraid so, ma'am."

I paused and looked away, mourning children I never knew.

I had an opportunity to help end it. And I would. This war had affected quadrillions of lives. The Queen Mother was correct. It was time for a reckoning.

"Are we really going to blow up Aratan, Commander?"

I glanced at Raibous lifting an eyebrow. Now that the secret was out, I wondered where it would lead. The crew was on a razor's edge.

"I don't know, Ensign, to be perfectly honest. Something devastating must occur to get the enemy's attention. What that's going to look like is up to the Admiralty and the Board of Directors. All I know is it's my mission to provide them that option and I'm for damn sure going to do it."

Raibous nodded thoughtfully. "Far too many souls have passed already."

His inflection was heartbreaking.

I didn't want to intrude so I redirected.

"So, what do you know about the AI onboard, Ensign?

Rabious smiled, happy for the distraction. "I don't think it's technically onboard. I believe Lieutenant Taito's A.I. is downloadable. He helps them run calcs for jump-wave calibration.

"He?"

"They call him Slim. It's an anagram but I can't remember for what. Anyway, he's a hoot. He cracks jokes. He talks shit to the lieutenants. It's hilarious. He says, 'What are you going to do? Court Marshal me?'"

"Sounds right up my alley. I didn't see him when I was there."

"Commander Nalwist doesn't like him. Slim gives him a hard time, too."

I laughed out loud. "Well now I really can't wait to meet him."

"You'll have to get the Lieutenant's permission, ma'am. He's the only one that knows how to load him."

"Not even Lam?"

"I don't think so. But they don't keep me in the loop. I'm new boot nobody."

"Got to start somewhere, kid. My best advice, your first year on a ship, you work yourself into the ground. It'll take a minute, but you'll get noticed. Keep your mouth shut and come promotion time you'll jump."

"My first assignment was escorting a science frigate to the Emdeli Nebula in a container tug. They're like a surfing house trailer. I was pissed. I had just earned my NMK. I was a combat pilot. But I sucked it up because all I had to do was fly. The scientists could offload their own equipment, so I didn't have to mess with them. It was nice. I ended up loving that trip. Nothing but time to listen to tunes, stare out at the stars and dream about the course of my life."

Raibous smiled. "How'd that turn out?"

I grinned from ear to ear. I liked this kid.

"I'll have to let you know. I'm still working on it. Anyway, I flew tugs for damn near three years before I was promoted to second lieutenant. As soon as I did, I was transferred to the NMK wing on Zuridan."

"Zuridan? This was before the war?" Raibous looked alarmed.

"Quite a bit actually."

"I'm sorry, Commander. It's just that you don't look like you're old enough to have been an officer before the war."

"Well, thank you, Raibous, you old smoothie. I appreciate that."

Raibous' cheeks turned a vibrant blue. He was blushing.

"I didn't mean offense, ma'am. I'm not good at guessing with humans. You age so slowly."

I reached over and tapped his shoulder. "Don't ruin the moment, Raibous, I thought we were getting cozy."

I loved the blushing blue.

Raibous bumped his head on the bulkhead darting away from me.

It was the best laugh I'd had in a while.

Funnier still when he eased back into the hatchway in full salute with Gevin standing in front of him. Gevin was trying his best not to grin.

"Dismissed, Ensign. I need a word with the commander."

Raibous looked relieved. "Yes sir."

"Track down Taito for me," I hollered, as he split through the hatch. "See when he can hook me up with Slim."

Raibous turned and grinned. "Yes, ma'am."

“Slim?” Gevin glanced at me questioningly.

“Lieutenant Taito’s AI program for the dropship. He’s a foul-mouthed smart ass.”

Gevin grinned. “I know someone like that.”

“Right? We’ll either get along or I’ll delete him. So, what’s up? You’re a long way from the bridge.”

Gevin smiled as he walked past me to drop down on the pilot’s couch. He ran his hands over the controls as he looked it over. “I wanted to see the dropship.”

He missed flying. I didn’t have to know him to see that. But that wasn’t the reason he was here.

“I also wanted to get your take on what the Queen Mother said.”

“There it is.”

Gevin chuckled. “Am I that transparent?”

“Not really. It is the hot topic.”

Gevin turned and looked at me. “So?”

“I agree with her, Gevin. This must end. It’s been thirty years. This whole arm of the galaxy is a mess. It’ll take decades to recover. Where I don’t agree is where she thinks the Ancients will get involved. The Ancients don't care. They could have wiped the Aratani out in a week if they wanted. We're not so important to them that they lifted a finger to help. So, I'm not holding out any hope that the bastards are going to cruise over and help mop up."

Gevin erupted in laughter. He jumped up out of the couch and roared. I was afraid he'd lost it. He grabbed me up in a big hug still laughing. "Oh, Nena Videt, how I have missed you. Only you could cut to the core of galactic politics so succinctly."

"Well, I did minor in Poli-Sci at the academy."

Gevin wiped his eyes as his laughter subsided. Then a double take. "Did you really? You never told me that."

I winked. "I did. It was a compromise I made with my father, so he'd let me apply. He hoped I would take to politics instead of becoming a pilot."

"I can see why. You do like to argue."

"Only in situations where it's best not to kick somebody's ass. I had to fly, Gevin. You know what I mean? I would have agreed to strip search Linawogs if it would've gotten me in a cockpit."

More laughter. He was slap happy from lack of sleep.

"Linawogs. You are too much, lady."

"I sure hope so."

Gevin took a deep breath, pulling himself together. There was more on his mind, but he hesitated to speak of it. I was just glad I could lighten his mood for a few minutes. He glanced around again before walking toward the hatch. I followed him out.

"I don't agree with the admiral's plan, Nena. It's not right."

The depth of his conviction was on full display in the depths of his fathomless green eyes.

I didn't know what to say. It was a hell of a thing to admit in the jam we were in.

"What's his plan?"

"Plan A is to destroy Aratan. Plan B is to take out the primary and waste the whole system."

That hit me hard. Kirpich wasn't playing around.

"Wow. That's heavy. A whole star system. Damn."

"Damn indeed. I can't believe that my father signed off on this. It goes against everything he stands for."

"He's tired of sending babies into the meat grinder, Gevin. Look at Ensign Raibous. All the marines in his class got shipped straight to sector five. How many of them do you think are still alive? How moral is it to keep feeding that machine?"

Gevin sighed. "I know. It's a damnable situation. But I must believe all races are equal. Genocide is not a solution. There's a better way."

I lifted an eyebrow. "Okay. What's your alternative?"

"I want to use the hyper matter to make smaller yield weapons and destroy them on the field. Minimal civilian casualties and our principles remain intact."

Gevin was a good and righteous man. I will always love him.

"We're way past that point. There's no way we could maintain that kind of pressure. The command structure is in tatters. Crews are growing mutinous, running from the fight. What I've learned these past few days is staggering. I read that the production planets can't maintain the levels of resources they're providing now. The whole system is about to collapse. This can't go on another year."

Gevin stared through me. He didn't like what he was hearing but it was the plain damn truth. "I'd forgotten how resourceful you were."

"I had to get caught up. It's not like I didn't just get dropped in the middle of a shit storm or anything. I had to know what I was up against."

Gevin's eyes turned the most haunted I'd ever seen them. "How's that working for you?"

"Honestly, I'm scared to death and that pisses me off."

"That's not the right fuel for the fire." Gevin wrapped his arm around my shoulders.

"No, but it's kept me alive this long. So, I'm going to go with that."

Gevin shook his head ever so slightly. He seemed disappointed.

"I just don't want you to miss the small joys in each day while you're busy being angry, Nena. It's no way to live, no matter the odds we're facing."

I sighed, sitting down on the hatch platform.

"Well, that's sure as hell going to be rough these next few weeks but I'll do my best."

"That's all you can do. So, you'll just have to haul it in, Mariner. I need you on point."

I giggled. "So did you steal all my best material or what?"

"No. Just that one. It always spoke to me. Where did you get it?"

"From my father. His view on peace. It was always part of his diplomatic party banter. He'd say, 'Peace doesn't bestow itself. You must haul it in.' It took me a while to gather his meaning but after the war started, I realized the same ethic applied to victory."

"Sounds like your dad was a fine man. His reputation as a diplomat was resplendent."

I grinned, thinking of my father and the shine on his big bald head in the morning before he assumed his wigs and parliamentary trappings. "He was a sweet man. I wish he was still here."

Gevin leaned forward and kissed me on the forehead. It meant the world to me.

"He did a wonderful job with you." He winked. "All things considered."

"I love you too."

Gevin smiled. "Alright well I will leave you to your duties, Commander. Remember, you have a standing invitation for dinner. I usually just eat alone in the mess."

"Cool. I'll buzz you when I wrap up here."

"Still no link?" Gevin frowned.

"I'm on the doctor's list. I'll have to have Taito for a few hours too, whenever I get in to see her. He'll have to calibrate it and get me hooked up in a simulator."

"Well, if you haven't heard from the doctor by first watch tomorrow let me know. I'll expedite things. I want you to be able to take the dropship out when we reach Bel Zari."

"The sooner the better. Some of the flight controls on this thing need tweaking. Maybe a few days' work. I won't know until I fly it."

"Is it bad?"

"No. Lam and Taito did a fantastic job. This thing is a step beyond. It's just that they're not pilots. They have some stuff in weird places from a regular cockpit."

"Ah, okay. Well, I will leave that to you, but keep me in the loop."

"Yes, sir."

Gevin put his hand on my shoulder. "These next few weeks may well be the stuff of history, Nena. We need to face it with a clear mind and joy in our hearts."

I nodded, fathoming the slipstream of time rushing toward us. "Or else why bother?"

Chapter 10

The ship lurched out of hyperspace as I lay face down, strapped, with my head in a vise waiting for Dr. Gillomi and Taito to get their shit together. It was a good thing that they weren't shoving nanofilament into my brain at the time.

I was nervous enough.

"The scan looks great, Commander." Dr. Gillomi patted my immobilized shoulder. "The extra time worked to our advantage. The bonds are even better than I hoped for."

"Cool. That makes me feel better. The old wiring was in there a long time."

"The technology has come a long way since the start of the war. And Lieutenant Taito's contributions are to be commended. His laddering system is a stroke of genius."

"Thank you, ma'am." Taito blushed. "I've worked hard on it."

"It is definitely one of a kind, Lieutenant."

"Well, that's great and all folks but can we move this thing along? My boobs are squished. I think one of them just fell asleep."

They chuckled as Dr. Gillomi brushed my hair aside to access the port.

"Won't take but a few minutes. Just need to get my camera threaded in with the lead here, and...."

I saw the light go on over top of me. I wished I could have seen what was going on, but nothing hurt so that was a good sign.

"Lieutenant, enhance the lower right corner of the grid."

I heard the doctor's breath fall shallow. She was hyper-focused.

"Yeah, that looks great. Almost done, Commander. Take a deep breath and relax."

I started counting the squares on the floor. Until I felt the ship dip to port.

"Damn it. What the hell is going on up there." Dr. Gillomi rested her hand on my shoulder until the ship levelled.

"Everything all right, Doc? I've come too far to have my brain scrambled now."

"You're fine. Commander. Just wasn't expecting that. It's not a good sign."

The alarm sounded general quarters. The staff around us scrambled.

"Nope." I bit my lip. "Doesn't sound like it."

Bel Zari was under attack.

It took a painstaking few minutes for the doctor to finish. The shields had taken a few hits in the interval, and I was starting to get antsy.

Finally, the bed rotated over. I was crazy relieved as gravity shifted and the restraints slipped away. I sat up and stretched, rotating my head.

"How do you feel?" Gillomi asked.

"I feel good. You nailed it, Doc."

Gillomi grinned. "Good. Well, Commander, you're cleared for duty. If you have any problems after you link up, reach out to me directly."

"Thank you. I do appreciate it."

"You're welcome." The doctor grasped my hand and leaned in close. "Just complete your mission, Commander. It's time for this to end."

I looked her dead in the eye. Her anguish was apparent. “Count on it.”

Taito and I skated the rush to the hanger decks and took the long way around to the lab. I wanted to be in a cockpit fighting. But the admiral wouldn’t allow it.

I needed to focus on my mission. If we ever managed to get there.

“You don’t have to waste time with me if there’s something you need to do, Lieutenant. I’ve waited this long. I can wait until after the ship blows up.”

Taito smiled. We were starting to get used to each other. I liked him.

“The captain said to stay with you until you’d run a few missions on the simulator and help reconfigure the controls. I’m yours all day, Commander.”

“Well, I will have to send Gevin a thank you. You’re the best present I’ve had in a while.”

Taito grinned. “You could do better, but you’d have to pay for it.”

I winked. “I never pay for it.”

A wild laugh burst out of him. It made me giggle too. He was a pleasant man, unguarded.

"You always end up paying for it." He grinned. "One way or the other."

I smiled; genuinely glad our paths had crossed along this crazy ride. "You're a wise man, Lieutenant."

Viginti's image appeared before me via my brand-new command crown. Taito had just gotten me hooked up and I jumped at her appearance.

"Commander, I've been trying to reach you."

I looked at Taito and rolled my eyes.

"I just now got my crown fitted, Viginti. You're my first call."

Taito grinned as he checked the link to the crown.

"The admiral needs you to report to blue sector and coordinate with the Zari liaison. We're taking on armor, supplies, and personnel as fast as we can and keeping the engines hot. Zari forces just repelled an Aratani carrier. Intel thinks they jumped out to await reinforcements. A Zari cruiser and support is taking over blue sector and the Admiral wants you to oversee it. Check in with me when you arrive."

Viginti faded before I could respond.

"Well, fuck, Taito, looks like we're not going to be in the simulator today. I have to go to blue sector and help with the bug out."

Taito raised an eyebrow. "Bug out? We just got here."

"The Zari just repelled an Aratani carrier. They think it's coming back with reinforcements."

Taito nodded. "We should probably bug out then."

"Right?"

"What do you want me to do while you're gone?" Taito asked.

"Oh, hell no. You're on my six, Lieutenant. I've got you for the whole day?" I winked. "You can help me bring order to chaos."

Taito nodded curtly but didn't look enthused.

"And get a good look at some Zarian technology."

That made him smile.

Blue sector was the home of the lost battleship. They'd barely had time to settle in before they were destroyed. The barracks had been cleared and cleansed. It looked brand new, as if no one had ever touched it.

It was eerie.

The first supply frigate entered the bay as we crossed the operations deck. Its hot shot pilot pitched it around a hundred and eighty just before touching down in the back of the bay.

"Nice parking job. Not her first day in the cockpit."

Taito grinned looking the ship over. "Even their supply ships look threatening."

I grinned. "I know, it's awesome, right? These ladies know how to throw down."

"That they do. And the intricacy of their nanotech is awe-inspiring. I'd give a month's pay to sit at the bench with a Zari designer."

"I won't charge you, Lieutenant. But you will have to wait until this madness is over."

We both spun around startled to find the Queen Mother and her retinue standing behind us. Man, they were some sneaky bitches. It was disquieting...and terribly fascinating.

I bowed my head. "Great Mother, we are honored."

The Queen Mother smiled. "You know Zuri protocol."

"Not in any great depth, Great Mother, but I'm all for any gal that likes to kick a little ass."

A light ignited in the Queen Mother's eyes as she burst into laughter, as did her retinue.

"Ah! Here, my children, is a huntress!" The Queen Mother chuckled. "What is your name, Commander?'

"Nena Videt, Great Mother."

"Nena! That is a fetching name, child. Where are you from?"

"Janus."

"Janus? Really?" The Queen Mother smiled. "There has to be a story there."

I grinned, shooting Taito a wink. "You have no idea, ma'am."

"Well, this is a tale I must hear. You will have to join me for dinner, Commander. I want to know about you and the Well project. Lieutenant, you're welcome to join us as well."

Taito smiled warmly, "It'd be an honor, Great Mother."

"Righteous!" The Queen Mother smiled, watching as her frigate pilots parked in neat rows across the bay. "If we survive this day, we'll have deserved it."

The Queen Mother was amazing.

She stayed at a mad dash beside me for sixteen straight hours as we unloaded, berthed, and stowed an entire legion of combat staff and an army of repair crews. I don't know what kind of deal she struck with Admiral Kirpich, but it was a historic event. It also put a welcome bit of bite into our dwindling options.

It was interesting to observe her in action. She knew all her huntresses by name. And it was apparent that her troops were enamored with her. They spoke with reverent respect, but their interpersonal exchanges were light-hearted and funny. They loved to laugh. It was a way more relaxed vibe than I'd imagined. These ladies were on point, knew their shit, and carried it out while laughing and singing songs. They were warriors in the purest sense of the word.

It was a privilege to be among them.

"Great Mother, do I have to be Zarian to be a huntress? I want to join your army."

The Queen Mother's laugh was loud and unguarded. Her troops smiled when they heard it.

"It hasn't happened yet, but I don't think anything in the Measure forbids it," she grinned. "The calm suits you, doesn't it?"

"Your troops are amazing. This is the best organized exodus I've ever encountered. I was prepared for total chaos."

"Me too." Taito struggled by with an armload of gear.

"To be a huntress is to be much more than a soldier. A huntress is a healer and a teacher, a weaver, a baker, a cobbler, a blacksmith, an architect, a carpenter, and an engineer. A huntress is a scholar in a lifetime of learning. We are a community wild for experience. We like to love and laugh and push the boundaries of what is possible."

I looked up at her and grinned. "So, what's the downside?"

"No males."

"Damnit."

The Queen Mother laughed again. "Exactly. But it is different for us. We are of tertiary gender."

"I'd heard that."

The Queen nodded. "It is common in insectoid species. We have brood females, protector females and males. It's been nothing but drama ever since."

I giggled. "I can well imagine."

The Queen winked. "The Oten-Zari, the O.G. huntresses, left our home world just over a thousand years ago after a great war nearly destroyed our numbers. The protectors at that time weren't prepared for an enemy from the skies and our world paid dearly. The brood clans sold out the Oten while suing for peace. Their fleet was slaughtered. They didn't want the returning protectors to gain power and oppose them."

"Damn, that's rough. So, the brood females had all the power?"

"Propagating a species has its perks, yes."

"Wow. So how did this schism come about?"

The Queen Mother grinned. "Schism. That's a fantastic word! And entirely apt. The first Queen Mother led our schism, Ardoo Adiin. She was the guardian of a field marshal killed in the trap. More importantly, she was a wealthy privateer who used her fortune to help the Oten at that time."

"So, the Oten became the Zari?"

The Queen Mother smiled. "The Oten were always Zari."

One of the Queen Mother's bodyguards chuckled. The queen glanced over at her with a grin.

"Okay, what am I missing?"

"Zari was a maligned Goddess. Her name eventually became an epithet hurled by breeders whose male was having sex with an Oten. I'll spare you the history lesson but in our society, it was a damning curse. In more modern times the Oten suffered at the hands of the breeders. Those who weren't protectors were either indentured servants or incarcerated. Their wild streak was an embarrassment in gilded times. After the massacre, Queen Mother Ardoo set about rallying the disenfranchised Oten to her cause, separation from the Yakaran state."

"Sounds like a bloody affair."

"Not as bad as you would think. The economic ramifications were devastating for the Yakara. The loss of the cheap Oten labor pool put them in a tailspin for years. I believe on Earth they call that poetic justice?"

“Same as on Janus,” I nodded.

“Well, anyway, now, a thousand years on, we have pretty much diverged as species, but we maintain a good relationship with the Yakara and thus with the Union.”

“Well, ma’am, I know I’m glad to have you ladies along. It’s been a hell of a ride so far.”

The Queen Mother sighed, turning to look out over the bustling flight bay. “I fear that ride is far from over, Commander.”

“Yeah, me too.”

The unsettled permutations of an unknown fate lingered.

“Is that the last frigate?” The Queen Mother lifted her arms to stretch. It was a graceful, flowing, movement. Her armor seemed to shimmer from the kinetic energy.

“Yes, ma’am. Your fighters are a go for landing as soon as it clears the bay.”

“Here they come.” Taito appeared behind me grinning like mad as the huntresses swooped in clad in their nanite armor.

Zarian armor was nothing less than a force of nature.

The nanites could change into almost any form of matter and constituent elements. It could be a short-range fighter, a knockout cocktail dress or a killing machine on the battlefield. The armor enhanced every aspect of the lethal Zari huntress.

"The Shun-Ja!" The Queen mother roared as they emerged in the hanger. "The huntresses of my tribe!"

The huntresses entered the bay and bowed before sitting on the deck in rows, prone. None of the other troops had done this so I was curious as to why her own tribe lay prostrate. Then, while I stood around wondering, the Queen Mother started howling with laughter as each rose to greet her in turn.

I came to learn that by sitting prone, they were playing a joke on the Queen Mother because she always left them waiting. They said she'd been this way since childhood.

The fire of pride was alive in the Queen Mother's eyes as she settled in among her family.

"If you don't need anything else, Great Mother, I'll leave you to settle in."

The Queen Mother wrapped me in a big hug. Her armor yielded instinctively. It felt like fabric.

"Thank you, Commander. You and the lieutenant have been invaluable. You'll both join me tomorrow for the evening meal? I must hear more about Nena the heathen mariner."

I grinned, staring into the controlled fury of her eyes. "That's what the captain calls me."

"Your captain is a rare soul. He's very thoughtful for a male. I like him."

"He is a good man. I've known him since he was a curly haired ensign that couldn't fly in formation."

The Queen Mother smiled. "Ah, the plot thickens! I am intrigued. I will have to make sure the captain joins us. I cannot wait to hear this tale."

I grinned. "I'll try not to disappoint you."

"Something tells me you have sass to spare."

I smiled again as Taito, and I started to walk away. "Brass, sass and, right now, a tired old ass. But at least I haven't been voided, yet. I look forward to dinner, Great Mother."

"As do I, Commander. Until tomorrow."

"Good night, ma'am."

Taito and I were halfway back to the lab when general quarters sounded again.

The Aratani were back. And this time, they brought hell with them.

Chapter 11

The ship shuddered violently, as Taito and I raced fully out to the lab. We'd taken several big hits in just a few seconds and the shields wouldn't bear it long. I felt the ship accelerate into a steep roll before the dampeners compensated.

"We're running."

Viginti appeared in my head's up as we jumped down the steps to the engineering deck. "Are you still in blue sector, Commander?"

"Negative," I gasped, a tiny bit winded. "We're headed for the engineering lab. I'm running on fumes here. What do you need?"

Taito and I dropped down another flight of steps onto the lab deck as the ship shuddered again. The shockwave sent Taito ass over tea kettle across the deck. To his credit, the crazy bastard rolled straight over on his feet and never broke stride.

A true Mariner.

"A diversion. The admiral and Queen Mother have a plan. Would you like to fly some drones?"

Somehow I found another gear to kick my ass up in.

"We're almost to the lab now."

Flying drones with my command crown finally in place was the next best thing to being there. The admiral had me take out three full squadrons to escort a Zarian shuttle to a specific set of coordinates close to the planet's equator.

The plan was to make them think that the Queen Mother was escaping the battle.

The trick worked as both Aratani cruisers broke off their attack to pursue us.

The Zari Huntresses were giving the Aratani carrier all it wanted. It didn't look like it would last long. Their energy weapons were fierce. I'd never seen such a tiny craft pack such a wallop. One squad had already made mincemeat out of the carrier's main flight deck. The second squad was doing the same to their bridge. The Huntresses were so small the Aratani batteries were totally ineffective. They were basically shooting at each other.

It was no surprise the Aratani risked an attack here. The Zari were the only thing keeping the Union in the game. I wondered if more Aratani ships were inbound.

Splitting her forces might not be to the Queen Mother's advantage.

Though, truthfully, there really wasn't much choice.

"Zari cruiser, accelerate to full speed. Looks like we got them to bite. Let's see if we can reel them in."

"Copy, Commander."

The voice sounded familiar. It sounded like one of the Queen Mother's guards. They were both formidable ladies.

I had the tail squadron of drones do a one-eighty and accelerate to attack speed on the lead cruiser. They were no match for its firepower but it feigned desperation.

The cruiser ignored the drones and took a long shot at the shuttle. Its pilot dodged easily then dropped into a steep dive for the planet's surface.

"Closing on coordinates now, Commander Videt. Sell it for about another ninety seconds then disengage. We have a surprise waiting for them."

Loonda. That was her name.

"Copy, Loonda, Thanks for the help."

"You can thank me when you see me again, Commander."

I smiled. There was so much I could learn from them. They were amazing.

"Let's not wait too long."

"Copy that," Loonda responded. "I'm out."

I sent the first squad to follow her to the atmosphere and then return to form on me. I had a minute or so to give the Aratani a little hell and I was going to take advantage.

The lead cruiser fired two massive volleys trying to hit Loonda's shuttle before it made the atmosphere. I jumped a few ships up into the line of fire and made for their engines. As I rolled around, I saw something shimmer in the atmosphere.

The Aratani pilots saw it too. The lead ship overrevved reversing engines and flamed out. Momentum carried it forward without slowing.

As I broke off and came around, I saw the light was coming from the planet's surface. I had a good feeling that was the Zari's 'surprise.'

It was time to break camp.

As I dashed full speed for the *Shaytan,* I focused both squad's gun cameras on the cruisers. I wanted to get good images of the Zari weapon in action.

I was about a hundred thousand klicks out when a blinding column of light emerged from the atmosphere. The lead cruiser ran headlong into it as it swept across the sky. It enveloped both ships like a spotlight but, as it faded back down into the atmosphere, there was no trace left of either cruiser. They both had been vaporized.

I had never seen a laser capable of that much firepower. I didn't even think it was possible.

But I had twenty cameras worth of footage as testimony.

The Queen Mother didn't play.

I had to boogie to catch up with the *Shaytan* as it was already cruising out-system. The Zari broke off their attack as the Aratani carrier turned to break free. But it was too late. The super-laser on the surface fired again and bisected the carrier.

The momentum from the engines propelled the aft section to quickly overtake and decimate the fore section. Its debris field shattered in fireworks behind me as I slid the squadron through the *Shayatan's* shields.

As soon as I set the drones on deck, the *Shaytan* jumped.

I clicked back over to my personal now and logged off-duty. Twenty hours was a good day. I was spent.

I looked up to find Taito bringing me a steaming bowl of something. It smelled amazing. My stomach growled in anticipation.

“How’d we do?” Taito asked, setting the soup and a tan colored roll in front of me.

I grinned taking the spoon from his hand. “You’re not going to believe the firepower the Zari have on that planet.” I slurped up a spoonful of soup. “Damn. What is that? That’s great!”

“Egg drop soup. My mother’s secret recipe.”

“Man, kudos to you and your momma. I could eat a liter of that.”

Taito grinned, taking the seat next to me. “I didn’t make that much. But there is more when you’re ready.”

I hammered on the soup before taking a big bite of roll. I was ravenous. “I recorded what it did to the Aratani cruisers on my way in. It vaporized them. Nothing left but ionized gas. It passed over them like a decontamination beam and then they were gone, atomized. It cut the damn carrier in half."

Taito's eyes widened in surprise. "Atomized them?"

I nodded solemnly. "You'll have to look at the footage. I can't even begin to calculate how powerful that thing is."

"Somewhere north of ten exawatts by my calculations."

I lifted an eyebrow and turned to Taito. "Who's that?"

"Slim." Taito grinned.

"At your service, Commander Videt."

"Well, nice to meet you, Slim," I glanced around the room. "So, really? Ten exawatts? That's insane."

"What will really warp your brain is that it wasn't technically a laser. It was a focused photon stream contained in an unbalanced plasma field. I'd venture that the total energy output was somewhere closer to 20 exawatts. Enough to power every planet in the Union for a day or so."

"Damn."

"Exactly," Slim replied.

Taito whistled as he abandoned his chair to grab more soup. "That's scary stuff. How do they generate that much power without melting the whole planet down?"

"I could make a few bucks off that answer." I winked at Taito, handing him my bowl.

"I'd venture that it goes hand in hand with their advanced nanotechnology." Slim loaded my gun camera footage of the blast on the holo-display over the table. "If they can indeed program their nanites to mimic any form of matter they could easily produce enough material to build it."

Taito nodded thoughtfully. He sat our bowls down and eased into his seat deep in thought.

"What are you thinking?" I slid my bowl over and dug in.

"The galaxy's a scary place, ma'am. Beings harnessing the power to destroy worlds? Should such a thing be our domain? Truthfully?"

I put my hand on his shoulder and nodded. The war had pushed everyone to the breaking point. We had to carry on because there was no longer a choice.

“I think it’s fair.” I shrugged before guzzling more soup. “If the Universe is going to leave our ass this far out in the breeze, she should provide a path out as well.”

Taito shrugged. His conviction was shaken. He sighed, staring into his soup as he stirred it. “There’s no way out but through, now. But how much longer will anyone have after that?”

I shook my head. I didn’t have an answer. I hadn’t dared think that far ahead.

“I get the vibe, guys. I do.” Slim spoke like a Gakkai conman. “But I am still a logical construct. I think it best we focus on the Commander’s mission and hope we’re still in one piece when we get there.”

“Copy that,” I yawned. Now that I’d eaten fatigue was creeping fast up on me. “I just hope we don’t have any more diversions.”

“Or encounters,” Taito stared mirthlessly into his bowl. “The Well must be set up in a very precise location. We will be vulnerable.”

“I feel a lot better having the Zari along.”

Taito nodded, a grin sliding across his face. “Hopefully, they’ll share some of their photon-plasma cannons. They’ll come in handy.”

Slim giggled. I'd never heard an A. I. giggle. He sounded charming.

"Yeah, I doubt it. But it is a nice thought."

"Do you think we could make one?" Taito was intrigued.

"Not at that wattage." Slim slid some power usage schematics up on the display. "But we might be able to make one a couple of hundred petawatts. I'll start a sub-routine to study it."

"Yes, please do. If it's practical it would create its own place in the arsenal. Great for close quarters ship to ship."

"True." I finished my last bit of soup and pushed the bowl back. "You could slide up under a carrier's belly and slice it open like swine. It didn't look like shields mattered."

"In the exawatt range it shorted them out. That may not be so at lower wattages. That is something to consider."

"Well, we will have to work on it another time." Taito got up to clear the table. "Tomorrow you two need to be in the simulator working on the control interface."

“What time do you want to start?” I got up from the table and stretched. My belly was full, and I was exhausted.

“I’m ready now.” Slim had this whole huckster vibe. It was hilarious.

Taito waved his arm dismissively. “You switch off and go to work on the plasma cannon. How’s 1500, Commander? That’ll give us a watch and a half to rest.”

“Perfect.” I yawned. “I’m going to sleep until it’s time to drop down.”

Taito grinned. “Don’t be late. I’ll have warm mochi in the morning.”

“I have no idea what that is but, if it’s as good as the soup, I’m in.

“Until the morning, Commander.”

I smiled and saluted a true new friend. “Goodnight.”

The crew was at a mad dash as I made my way up to the hive. I had to dodge a crew of oncoming techies as I stepped off the lift. I was so tired I felt like I was walking underwater. I tried to stay out of the way and meandered into the tram stop feeling every day my age. I stepped onto the tram with a bunch of flight techs just coming off duty. As I stepped forward to make room inside, I saw Gunny Tropa, along with his back-up singers, Nok and Enu, standing at the front of the car.

The big bastard grinned when he saw me. I rolled my eyes in contempt and turned away.

I knew he was coming before I heard him lumber across the deck.

He was too stupid not to.

“Well, if it isn’t the admiral’s catamite. How are we this evening, Commander?”

I turned ever so slowly to look up at his big ugly face. I raised an eyebrow, making my displeasure apparent. “Catamite? Wow. That’s a big word for you, gunny. I’m impressed. Too bad you don’t know what the hell it means.”

The look of confusion on his big dumb face was worth having to smell his breath.

“You could be the admiral’s catamite.” I grinned. “Though, I would think him of terrible taste, if so.”

Tropa snarled and I couldn’t help but giggle. I was totally exhausted, but I wasn’t taking any of his shit.

"One day soon your mouth's going to override your ass, convict."

"One day soon I'll have you shot for malicious insubordination, Gunnery Sergeant. You want to go ahead and get it over with?"

The flight techs around us clearly did not. They quickly created a wide berth in the crowded car.

Tropa glared at me for a long second before glancing around at all the potential witnesses. I still didn't credit him with enough brains to chill out, though.

And apparently neither did the invisible Zari guard who'd been tailing me.

Everyone in the car gasped collectively as her nanite cape transformed and she appeared, in full force, beside me.

Damn, they were impressive.

Tropa's eyes widened like he'd seen the devil himself. His fear was real.

"Tell me, Commander, are all your enlisted so impertinent?"

I turned to glance at the huntress but didn't recall her face. I grinned and winked out of the gunny's view.

"No, thankfully not, My Huntress. Gunny Tropa here is a very special case. He thinks his own dick holds more weight than the chain of command or the Mariner Tenets. He would not have a place in my command."

The gunny seethed but held his tongue as the huntress gave him a close once over.

"A problem common among males of most species, I'm afraid. All balls and no brain." The huntresses circled Tropa stating her assessment. His discomfort was glaringly hilarious. "It's a quirk of evolution, I suppose. The trait survives though it's clearly a dead end."

"A paradox?" I grinned.

The huntress gave the gunny a quick sniff before moving away. "More syllables than he's worth, it seems."

Tropa stood staring, completely disarmed. I grinned at the huntress before turning to wave dismissively. "You're dismissed, Gunnery Sergeant. Don't cross my path again."

Tropa looked past me at the huntress before scurrying away. He was scared to death.

It was awesome.

"The Queen Mother requests that you stay with the Zari contingent. She was impressed with you, Commander, and wants to show her appreciation for your helping get us settled."

I smiled. At that moment I didn't care where I slept. I was beat. "I'd be honored."

Chapter 12

I woke up in a cocoon.

Yeah, let that sink in... *a cocoon.*

I vaguely remembered climbing into what I thought was a rucksack. I was so damned tired I didn't care. It was just the inner liner for a cocoon or something equally nasty. I found myself naked, covered in ooze and struggling to catch a glimpse of light as I fought to break free.

As I lay flopping about, a couple of younger Zari arrived to help. I slid out and onto my feet, shaking and completely freaked out, covered in a bloody amber ochre.

It smelled revolting.

The pair toweled me off crudely then led me to a portable wash station. The sudden blast of warm sudsy water took a bit of shock out of the awakening.

What the hell had they done to me? I very much doubted they slept like this every night. What was the point? I made a mental note to hit up Dr. Gilomi if I didn't get an exemplary answer.

I stepped out of the shower to find towels and a robe along with my uniform cleaned and pressed. My command crown was sitting deactivated on top of it. I hadn't thought to check it.

I worried about a bit of funny business there, too.

I didn't like thinking this way. These ladies had been nothing but kind to me and were exemplary warriors. After everything I'd been through it had become instinct to suspect the worst, first.

There was no disgrace in being cautious.

"The Queen Mother wishes to see you as soon as you're dressed, Commander."

The two girls stood by under the guise of tinkering with equipment while I dressed.

I might have bought it if they weren't giggling.

They just wanted to see a human woman naked. It wasn't the worst thing.

They were cute, too.

The Queen Mother sat at the head of a huge table with her guards and huntresses gathered around her. The Zari utilized a low round table surrounded by pillows to sit on. The pillows and table dressing were pure white bordered with an iridescent turquoise that was stunning. For a bivouac setup it was gorgeous, fitting for a queen.

As I moved closer, I saw Lieutenant Taito talking to one of the huntresses. He grinned and waved when he saw me. He looked like he was having fun.

"Ah, Commander. I'm glad you could join us. I was starting to worry about you."

I shot the Queen Mother a puzzled look as I was shown a seat opposite of her. "How long was I out?"

"A standard day. The cells hardly ever hold anyone that long."

"Cells?"

"A Naris healing cell, they're a genetically modified parasite that regenerates cells while consuming their detritus. You, young lady, must have had loads of detritus to be held in thrall that long."

"Interesting." I accepted a glass of pale-yellow tea. "I just had a bio reboot a few days ago."

The Queen Mother scoffed. "They only fix what's wrong with you now. The Naris cells fix everything that ever went wrong in the system. Think of it as a reboot of your DNA."

"Well, I appreciate it, Queen Mother. I do feel well."

The Queen Mother smiled. She was holding something back. It felt like she was sizing me up. "I'm sorry I delayed your training further, Commander, but I thought it important. Lieutenant Taito was telling us of your difficulties getting started."

"It's been a comedy of errors, to be sure." I winked at Taito. "I guess now that my DNA's been re-booted, I'll be ready to throw down."

"Indeed." The Queen Mother stood, smiling, before walking around the table. "We are counting on the success of your mission, Commander. I am committed to doing everything possible to see that you are protected and prepared."

I stood and turned toward her approach. "I am honored, Great Mother. I'm all for anything that'll spike the odds."

The Queen Mother stopped before me and rested her hands on my shoulders. "Good. Because the path ahead will be tough. I have discussed it with my Council and Kin, we have decided to train you as a huntress."

I was thunderstruck, my thrill immeasurable.

I was also profoundly confused.

"Will I have time to prepare for both? We have less than a week."

"There is plenty of time if we use each second wisely. Time is a valuable asset when interfaced correctly. That is something you will learn."

The comment was a bit esoteric for me, but okay, whatever.

If I managed to survive this damn war being a Zari Huntress might not be a bad gig. I could do a lot worse. I looked up at the Queen Mother. Her excitement was apparent. It was contagious. "Where do we begin?"

"With a feast!" The Queen Mother's voice resonated through the room. I grinned ear to ear. Her enthusiasm was refreshing. "We must celebrate the new day ahead. Then, we will get you prepared for your flight training."

She led me to the head of the table to sit at her left hand.

It was terrifying.

The huntresses were intimidating in repose. Seeing the Queen Mother's inner circle was a jolting experience. That I could walk among them was inspiring.

I felt wholly undeserving.

"Lieutenant Taito was telling us about your dropship just before you got here, Commander. I find the whole concept intriguing. Though I must admit wondering about the quirk of contact with these Antithessians. My species has been spacefaring for over a millennium, and we have never encountered anything like them."

I shrugged. "I didn't know anything about them until I arrived here. I just flew my missions and somehow managed to gain the captain's attention."

"And I was so discourteous as to bring you right into the heart of the storm."

I looked up to see Gevin standing across from us. I beamed. "And I've never been more thankful."

Gevin smiled as he took a seat opposite the Queen Mother. "I trust no one more. Thank you for your invitation, Queen Mother. I had heard your morning feasts were exquisite."

"Eat your fill, Captain. The Zari start the day sated, loved and grateful for another chance to know the Universe."

"A commendable way to live, Queen Mother. I salute you." Gevin looked a tad uneasy around the huntresses, too.

It was a sense of good old-fashioned evolutionary prey instinct. We were decidedly not the apex predators in the room.

"I have become quite taken with your Commander Videt, Captain. She is a well-rounded, clever, Mariner. I may just keep her."

Gevin's grin was glowing. I didn't want to guess what he was thinking.

"She is definitely one of a kind, Great Mother."

"Why, thank you, Captain. That's so very nice of you to say." Gevin didn't have to know me to catch the sarcasm. But he knew me well enough to understand the tone, too; 'You'll pay for that later.'

His grin confirmed it. "You're welcome, Commander. So, you were discussing your mission?"

"We were pondering the Antithessians," The Queen Mother smiled. "By way of analysis."

Wow. She was good. Gevin looked suddenly uncomfortable. He shifted on his pillow and glanced at me.

I wasn't saving him. I wanted to know what he knew too.

"It is a peculiar phenomenon, to be sure, Great Mother. I'm not without questions myself. But I can only do as ordered. Command has a tight squeeze on this."

"So, what do you know, Captain?"

Gevin glanced from the Queen Mother to me. I raised my eyebrows, inquisitively. There wasn't any point in holding anything back. I was sure she'd know it.

"About eleven years ago a deep space listening post near D'Noii picked up a signal coming through hyperspace. The carrier wave was so powerful it fried the station's receivers. When the signal was finally able to be analyzed, they realized it was a data dump of several thousand xenottabytes of information."

Murmurs sounded around the table.

"The full schematics for the Well, all its circuitry, the original dropship and its storage matrix were in that transmission. Along with transmission frequencies to contact them for the exchanges."

The Queen Mother furrowed her brow. "They contacted the Union specifically?"

"Intelligence didn't think so at the time," Gevin shrugged. "The wave was strong enough to have easily gone on to the opposition quadrants, maybe even extragalactic."

"A message in a bottle?"

Gevin grinned at me. "So, it would seem. They didn't care from whom they received the hydrogen from as long as they got it."

"And your Board of Directors just took this at face value?" the Queen Mother asked.

"Oh, there's been a ton of conjecture among the command staff about how all that went down." Gevin shook his head. "No one knows what else was in that original transmission, but something got them on the march. Work began on the Well at Starbow barely a year after the transmission was received. It was so sophisticated it took nearly nine years to complete."

"That place is a rat trap."

Gevin nodded solemnly. "I'm sorry you ever had to go there, Nena. It's not our finest hour."

The Queen Mother ran her hand down a braided lock of her palatine hair. "So, what is the Union doing with all of that power? We've seen no evidence of it, aside from this ship."

Gevin nodded. "That's the other thing that has tongues wagging. We had hoped that some power would be routed to help boost manufacturing. The fleet is taking a beating that it can't bounce back from. And they've done nothing."

"They've put that much weight on this mission?" The Queen Mother looked skeptical.

"It would appear so, Great Mother."

I saw the weight of it in Gevin's eyes. He was telling the truth.

The Queen Mother nudged my shoulder. "I guess you better not screw this up, huh?"

Nice! I giggled like a stupid schoolgirl. "Probably wouldn't be a good idea."

"Well, if anything does go wrong it won't be because we weren't prepared." The Queen Mother raised her glass. "I will be taking charge of your training personally."

That quieted the room down.

Gevin lifted an eyebrow. "Training?"

I shot him my most mischievous grin. "The Queen Mother is training me to be a huntress."

I couldn't tell if he was going to laugh or shit. He looked terribly uncomfortable.

"The Admiral agreed to let me help the Commander prepare for her mission. This is my contribution," the Queen Mother smiled.

It was disarming.

Gevin got the message. He nodded, glancing over at me. I read his expression.

Are you sure you know what you're doing?

"I'm dancing as fast as I can, my Captain." I winked.

"Our training will increase her odds dramatically, Captain. I have no doubt that the Commander will excel in this. She has the mind of a huntress."

"Thank you, Great Mother."

"Hush child."

I grinned. I was glowing.

"I have no doubt." Gevin smiled. "And that she is in great hands, Queen Mother."

Gevin grabbed another sweet roll from the table before standing. "I will leave you to it, then. There will be a briefing at week's end about system insertion. The operational tempo will be intense so bear that in mind when you're working."

"Roger that, sir." I nodded.

"Lt. Taito, keep me informed of the Commander's progress."

I chuckled watching the Lieutenant struggle to finish chewing a juicy mouthful of fruit before he could answer. His face reddened from the effort.

"Copy, sir."

"Good," Gevin smiled. "With a little luck we may get out of this intact."

"We're on the path of peace. As long as that is so, no departure is unworthy."

The Queen Mother's words hung tangible among us.

She stood, bowing slightly toward Gevin, who returned the gesture.

As he walked away the Queen Mother tossed a pearling to me from the table.

"Are you ready to get started?"

The Queen Mother's eyes stared through me. Her countenance was terrifying.

I stood holding her gaze. I could almost see my future in their depth. It was a moment of complete terror and total elation.

"I could not be more so, Great Mother."

Chapter 13

The next few days passed in wavelengths of time I had never thought possible. My whole sense of reality had been totally skewed. I'd thought the Queen Mother was being cryptic when she spoke of interfacing with time. But these chicks did it.

It was mind-blowing.

Their nano-armor had a neurological uplink a lot like a standard Union command crown. But their system could change how the huntresses perceived the passage of time, among other things. Their incredible reflexes and response times were due, in part, to a perceived slowness of time as well as an enhanced neuro-physical response from the armor.

When one could race full tilt through a world at half speed, it gave a whole new meaning to running amok.

Thus, our current game; Aki-voll. Also known as pummel Nena.

The rules were simple. I had a whole empty recreation deck to avoid the huntresses and their maidens from pummeling me with zero g Aki-volls. They were hand-sized ovoids which could be hurled a good clip past a hundred kph. They transmitted one hell of a shock through the armor.

After a few embarrassing rounds I was getting better. I dodged the opening salvo with only a glancing blow as I advanced on their line. But they were doing a skillful job of keeping me about twenty meters out.

I was getting frustrated.

"Find your path, Commander, and commit to it. Keep your eyes on it and move through space to get there. You're a pilot. You must think three dimensionally."

The Queen Mother's voice commanded the room.

Her comment struck a chord.

I was just running straight at them, like a big dummy, dancing around to avoid being hit. I needed to come at them from odd angles. Do the unexpected just like in a dogfight. I needed to find the weak spot.

I found it between the two shield maidens who stayed to gawk at my naked ass fresh out of the cocoon, Bootah and Ostobah. They were laughing at me more than anything and neither had lobbed a decent Aki-voll yet. The problem was to their left, Nashumi.

She was a newly consecrated huntress and deadly. She had striking, deep set emerald eyes and didn't say much. She had knocked me slick off my feet in an earlier round with an Aki-voll straight to the chest.

It took a minute to get my wind back. But she ran to help me as I did. All was good.

She was just intimidating.

I dashed for Bootah just as Nashumi hurled her Aki-voll. It curved to my right, so I dropped rolling left as it passed overhead. I sprang to my feet pulling my knees up and leaping as two came in to catch my roll. I soared up and over another one as I found a rhythm.

The radical movements kept the huntresses out of synch. They were targeting where I was. I did a backflip in the air and landed at a dead run, grinning as a slow expression of horror crossed Bootah's face. She froze realizing she was about to get mowed over.

Another Aki-voll whizzed in at shoulder height so I dropped to my knees and slid straight into her, taking her legs out. The Aki-voll she'd held in her hand landed on her chest and lit her up. She hadn't earned her armor yet and those things packed a wallop. She convulsed on the floor a few times as the Aki-voll discharged. It looked painful.

I took a deep breath as I retracted the armor's helmet and glanced around. It was ugly, but I made it.

"Very good, Commander. Now you have a clearer picture. They do come in quickly, don't they?"

"It's weird. You have time to decide, to execute a move, but you must be decisive, there's no time for second guessing."

The Queen Mother came to us as I helped Bootah to her feet and dusted her off. She wrapped the girl in a hug.

"There's never time for second guessing," the Queen Mother bellowed. The huntresses and maidens turned to face her. "A huntress must trust her intuition implicitly. As you place your trust in it, you will see that it, too, will gain confidence in you. Once that relationship thrives it will serve you well the rest of your days."

She looked down at Bootah slack in her arms. "Are you all right, my child?"

Bootah was pale. "Yes, Great Mother, thank you."

"You froze as the Commander closed in on you. Why?"

Bootah's expression saddened me. The mere question was a chastening.

"I second guessed myself, Great Mother. My instinct was to jump. But it made no sense as she was still on her feet. I thought I could hit her and knock her back. By the time she dropped it was too late to do either."

The Queen Mother nodded. She stroked the girl's face and smiled at her. "Now is the time for you to start forming a relationship with your intuition, little Bootah. It will quickly cease to speak to one who refuses to listen."

The girl nodded solemnly, in awe of the Queen Mother's attention.

"And you can take solace in the fact that the Commander is a shrewd warrior. I told her to pick a path, and like lightning, she picked the one of least resistance. She did not hesitate."

I blushed. "Thank you, Great Mother."

The Queen Mother winked at me before moving on. "Victory on a battlefield is gained by finding weak points and exploiting them. This may be accomplished a million different ways, but the underlying principle must be ever present in your mind."

"No problems. Only puzzles and solutions." This missive came from the Queen Mother's sister, Elora.

"Puzzles and solutions." A chant from the crowd.

It summed up the Zarian outlook on life. They didn't stress about anything. They seemed to float above the cesspool the rest of us paddled through. It was a mindset I could give myself over to.

But it wouldn't be easy. There were tons of old conditioning and data stuck in there.

"Now, it is time we let the commander get to her flight training," The Queen Mother settled Bootah on her feet.

I grinned as it was agreed, with a great deal of laughter, that the girls wanted to pummel me some more.

The Queen Mother smiled. They had taken me into the fold. "I have a new game for you. Let's see if we can help Bootah get in touch with her intuition."

Bootah's ears shot up. The sudden shock on her face was hilarious. The group fell apart with laughter. But, as I understood it, it was a momentous occasion. It would be Bootah's first lesson in earning her armor.

I patted Bootah on the shoulder as I headed for the hatch. “Just go out there and have fun, lady. It’ll keep you from over thinking.”

“Thanks, Commander.” She didn’t look at all convinced.

“There’s more training awaiting you too, Commander.”

I stopped and turned, grinning as I looked up at the Queen Mother. “Your challenge, Great Mother?”

The Queen Mother smiled warmly. She had my trust. I deferred to her as her subject.

“Nashumi thinks she can beat you up to the engineering lab. I wagered her that you would finish less than a meter behind.”

I scowled. “Behind?”

The Queen Mother’s smile was sly. “Prove me wrong.”

I didn’t say anything. I just grinned.

I glanced over at Nashumi. Her emerald eyes lit up at the challenge. I settled in beside her bent to the task.

"I've got you on my heads up, children." Elora activated her wrist top display. "Nashumi, show the commander how our armor really works."

Nashumi's smile was feral. She glanced at me as her green eyes glowed. "Try and keep up, sweetie."

"Just make sure you're going the right way." I winked.

And in that instant of confusion, I dashed from the room.

The Queen Mother's laughter roared behind me.

I sped down the deck at crazy speed. It took a few sliding turns to get used to the bursts of acceleration. But I was giggling like a baby. It was exhilarating.

Nashumi was hot on my six as we left the blue sector to cross over into Marine territory.

They were taken quite by surprise.

Nashumi and I leapt to scamper across opposite walls to avoid a group in the passageway. As we scaled the corners racing toward the inner hull, I saw Gunny Tropa coming out of his company office.

I grinned as I dropped onto the deck.

Tropa whirled around at the sound of me touching down. By the time he reacted I had already passed him at about seventy kph after having smacked his big dumb ass.

I don't know if it hurt or not but it sure as hell sounded like it.

Messing with the gunny did cost my lead. Nashumi stayed full bore along the bulkheads racing above traffic. I leapt up behind her and focused on closing the gap.

The nanite armor was an absolute marvel. I had barely scratched the surface of its potential. It understood one's intuition. There was a nodal interface for the computer, but it was useless on the fly like this.

You had to will stuff into being.

I started by copying Nashumi's four-legged form of propulsion. It was wildly efficient. The armor adapted perfectly to my smaller stature and short chubby arms. I was nowhere near the size and power of a huntress, but I was learning that it gave me an edge in maneuvering.

Once I got my nano arms under me it was off to the races.

We burst into the tram station overhead of the crowd and leapt across the platform to climb the decks of the inner hull. A security team took a couple of shots at us as we swung around the rail. They weren't even close to hitting us. We were cruising.

As I struggled to catch Nashumi an idea dawned. To get to the engineering deck we need to go five decks up and four blocks aft. As Nashumi headed straight up, I decided to head aft first.

There was a crossover bridge on this deck making it easier to cross. I could climb the decks inside that station.

As I dashed off, I wondered if Nashumi was aware. She stayed on her path and quickly went out of sight as I raced down the hull between decks. I was fatigued but the thrill of the moment and the fun of operating the armor kept me balls to the wall as I closed in on the skybridge.

As I climbed to the top and started up I saw Nashumi racing toward me from above. She was hauling ass.

I reached down deep and poured on my last bit of moxy to dash up the length of hull.

As I dropped around the rails into the station, Nashumi was hot behind me. I leapt to the hatchway and sped toward the Tech Corp lab.

As I dropped to the deck before the door, winning! Nashumi dropped to the deck and disengaged her helmet. She looked at me with a wicked grin and bowed her head slightly.

I tried to smile but I was busy sucking oxygen into my screaming lungs.

Nashumi didn't even look winded. She'd been instructed to let me win.

She glanced along the ground gauging the distance between us. She grinned. "Looks close enough to a meter to me."

I smiled back. "Thanks for letting me win."

Nashumi nodded. "The Queen Mother often says that you must be open to lessons presented beyond your focus. It doesn't matter who wins. You know how to run four-legged on walls now. How cool is that?"

I giggled. "Yeah, I didn't think I would be doing that today. Or any day."

"Just remember the honor and responsibility that comes with that armor, Nena Videt. Never take it lightly."

I nodded solemnly, standing my full height to look Nashumi in the eye. "I am honored that the

Queen Mother has taken me into her graces. You have no idea what it means to me. In the middle of this cosmic fucking mess, you gals are a light in my life. I don't take that lightly."

Nashumi smiled. "It is a great puzzle that our paths have crossed amid all this. Your soul is Zari, Nena Videt. It doesn't matter where you're from or where you've been. You're one of us now."

I started getting misty. "Thank You, Nashumi. It means the world to me."

Nashumi looked misty too. "Now go. Prepare for your mission. It's time this madness ends."

"I am all over it, sister. I'll see you tonight."

Nashumi winked before cloaking herself and shimmering away across the deck.

I smirked. "You got to show me that one."

Nashumi's response issued from my audio array. "It's in the main menu, commander. Looks like you need to spend more time studying. We'll discuss that later."

"Hey, it's only my third day." I hollered down the passageway. "I thought I was doing well."

Nashumi's giggle lingered in my thoughts the rest of the day.

Chapter 14

I tried not to look too terribly happy as I strolled into the admiral's briefing room. I already knew I was in the soup for racing Nashumi's to the tech deck. I'd hoped the Queen Mother would have smoothed things over. But as the admiral laid eyes on me, I saw that if she had it hadn't worked.

He really did not look happy.

Not, at all.

"Ah, Commander Videt, nice of you to take a leisurely stroll up top instead of terrorizing everyone along the way."

I grimaced. "Yes, sir."

"If the Queen Mother hadn't sanctioned that little stunt, you'd be in the brig right now. Are we clear, Commander?"

"Crystal, sir."

"Gunny Tropa's still in the med bay having his ass reconstructed." His face reddened. He was livid. "What in the name of infinite were you thinking?"

"I just wanted to give him a bit of quick encouragement. He's been so welcoming."

The admiral's glare was heavy.

I was a big toe over the line but, truthfully, with Tropa, I didn't regret it.

After a long few moments, the admiral smirked. I know he saw the humor in it. But the Tenets must be adhered to, at the very least in decorum.

"Well, this thing with you two ends now. I've sent word to Tropa, too, through his C.O. We have too much at stake for this pettiness. I expect better of you."

"I do apologize, sir. It was childish of me. I got caught up in the rush. This armor is unreal."

The Admiral looked me over.

The gunmetal gray liquid suit looked innocuous enough now, resembling a flight jumper. It was form-fitting but comfortable like a second skin. It could turn heads or bust them up. It was thrilling. I felt wild.

"What can it do?"

I paused feeling the tiniest bit smug. I took a deep breath and let the moment pass. The Queen Mother would not approve.

"It's a complete entity, Admiral. Its transformative and transubstantiate capabilities are only limited by the huntress's imagination. The onboard computer blows away anything in the fleet. And, it has archives from times before humans or even Jenadiin evolved. Some of the Ancient races were still corporeal then."

Kirpich nodded gravely pondering it. Then, slowly, he grinned. "And it lets you run along walls."

I grinned too. "Yes sir. It forges atomic bonds through a static charge that shuts down and fires several thousand times a millisecond. You are bound to the surface, but it doesn't hinder movement. In fact, it can be used in a limited way to enhance acceleration and maneuvering."

"Incredible."

"The Queen Mother and her huntresses are a marvel, sir. Absolutely deadly in battle and completely calm, loving, and present in repose. They laugh more than any beings I've ever encountered. They are a joy to be around."

"Warriors, all," the Admiral agreed. "I'm glad they've taken you under their wing. They are a true and just race. Just don't forget who signs your paycheck."

I lifted an eyebrow, grinning. "I'm getting paid? That's awesome!"

Kirpich chuckled. "Just don't sit around and wait for it to post. Accounting this mess may take years."

I winked. "As long as I'm around to collect, I don't care."

Kirpich motioned for me to sit as Gevin, Viginti, and several, until now, nameless advisors rolled in. Marine Lt. Colonel Tylus Jai and Magisters Impera Motai and Hollis Gaspalla.

Lt. Colonel Jai was a striking being. He looked tough as nails. A long, crooked, scar across his left cheek only emphasized his rugged good looks. He nodded graciously as he moved to sit next to Kirpich.

He was Tropa's commanding officer. I bet that pansy didn't give this guy any shit.

Gevin sat to the Admiral's right, grinning as our eyes met. He raised an eyebrow. *'Having fun?"*

I grinned from ear to ear, nodded my head and winked. *'You better fucking believe it.'*

Gevin grinned, shaking his head as he activated a terminal pad.

A view of the entire Anowi system formed at the center of the conference table. It was a completely dead system with a couple of fast-moving gas giants blazing close to the primary star and four big dead boulders way out system safe from the touch of the gas giants' gravity. As Gevin narrowed the scope of the projection, Commander Lund, along with Nalwist and Taito, slipped in the door followed shortly by the Queen Mother and Elora.

Lund slipped into the chair next to me nodding cordially.

"Alright, folks. We are less than twelve hours from egress into the Anowi system." Gevin narrowed the view of the holo again to take in the orbit of the largest dead world.

"This is our destination, Vostom. It's a dense heavy gravity world. It absorbs electromagnetic signals like a sponge and will help hide the Well and the ship from long range sensors. We will set up a heliocentric orbit on the light side of the planet for maximum benefit. Once there, things will move quickly. We want to be in and out in less than twenty hours."

That timetable raised eyebrows, especially mine. That predicated on a whole lot of things going right. I wasn't sure if that was hope or desperation.

Gevin noted it as he glanced around the room. "How quickly after achieving orbit can the Well device be ready, Commander Nalwist?"

The funky chicken hopped from his chair to speak. "We will be ready to run the first mission within ninety minutes of arrival. Powering it up the first time will take the longest. After that, it is just a matter of ten minutes or so for the follow ups."

"Are we set up with the Anithessians to run two missions on the first rotation?" the Admiral asked.

"We are." Nalwist nodded. "They have two more loads ready to go as well. A benefit of our delay it seems."

Kirpich glanced over at me. "Feel like flying four missions?"

I smirked. "Let me live through the first three and we'll see how it goes."

"Fair enough." The Admiral grinned.

"How is your training going, Commander?" Gevin looked bemused.

"I have the ship down cold. It's a great piece of machinery." I winked at Taito. "I've done well against the conditions in the simulation right up to the point where Olankampf bites it. There was no place he could have gone. It may be that there aren't many breaks in the energy streams there. I really can't make an educated guess because I can't see past the end of his data."

"But the flow changes constantly. The conditions now could be completely different." Gevin toggled through the readings on the display.

"Exactly." I looked him in the eye. "For better or worse. Some deep points are just too wild to fly, let alone try to dive through."

"Well, in any case, Commander, you're about to find out. So, let's come at it with a bit of optimism and see what happens." The Queen Mother patted my hand.

"No problems. Only puzzles and solutions."

The Queen Mother glowered. "Try to let that sink in."

I cast my gaze down, subservient. "Yes, Great Mother."

It wouldn't be easy. I was a dyed in the wool pessimist. But I couldn't disappoint her. I knew I wanted things to change.

I needed to change.

"Now, what's our plan for C.F.P?" Gevin asked.

Commander Lund cleared his throat before speaking. "I've coordinated with Huntress Elora, and we have devised a three-pronged defense that'll keep us from stretching ourselves too thin."

Kirpich leaned forward in his chair. "What do you have in mind?"

Lund glanced at Elora to defer. She smiled and waved her hand. "It's your plan, Commander. And a good one. I just want to keep my girlies safe."

Lund smiled. Elora's charm was disarming.

"Our plan is to drop off four squads of huntresses just beyond heliopause as soon as we exit. They will set up passive listening posts and only chime in if necessary. Then, when we make orbit, we deploy the new A.I. drones to patrol the entire outer system with each squad maintaining a quadrant for rapid response to a breach."

I hadn't really paid attention to Viginti lingering over Kirpich's shoulder but, when Lund mentioned the A.I drones, I saw her flinch.

Her face was pure horror.

Were they seriously hacking up hybrids to fly drones? That was creepy. It reeked of desperation.

It also leaned hard on the Tenets.

"Why are we deploying the A. I.'s?" Gevin asked.

The question was asked of Kirpich, not Lund.

Gevin felt it leaning too.

"The planet, sir." Lund looked uncomfortable. "We won't be able to maintain a control signal. And we need to remain as emission free as possible."

Gevin nodded, seeing the logic. He wasn't at peace with it, though.

"What's the third prong, Commander?" Kirpich sat up in his chair.

He hadn't so much as glanced at Gevin since asked about the A.I.

Something was up there.

Lund's concern was apparent. He was easy to read.

"We will maintain two NMK squads on four-hour rotations. It will keep them sharp and, if something happens, we will still have plenty of fresh pilots to launch."

Kirpich nodded enthusiastically. "So ordered, Commander. Good job."

Lund nodded in deference with a quick glance at Gevin. "Thank you, sir."

It wasn't the first time Kirpich had muddied the waters in the chain of command. And Gevin, being the exemplary mariner he was, wouldn't let it carry long.

Great. Something else to worry about.

"Well, alright, I think everyone is up to speed." Gevin rose. "The ship will remain in general quarters for the duration. I do not want to get caught flat footed. Keep your troops fresh, fed and on point. Rotate shifts as you wish. It's going to be a long day."

Kirpich stood as the crowd poised to rush out. "I know I don't have to tell you the stakes but keep them in mind these next few hours. This is our shot. We can't let it escape us."

That put a chill in the room. No pressure there.

"Dismissed."

I lingered in my seat waiting for the crowd to thin. Taito winked at me as he followed Nalwist out. Lund, in a blazing display of emotion, patted my shoulder once before walking away. But really, it moved me. He was a good man. He just wasn't emotionally demonstrative.

Like most males.

The Queen Mother struck up a lively conversation with Gevin and escorted him from the room. Elora stopped at the doorway and whistled at me. "C'mon, Videt, you're on guard."

I grinned, rising from my seat. "I didn't want to be presumptuous and intrude."

Elora smiled as I joined her at the door. "You're in the Queen Mother's retinue now. You stay with her any time she's out."

"Yes ma'am."

Elora leaned close as we followed along. "We need to get into this A.I. thing."

As we passed a corridor, I saw Viginti engaged in a lively conversation with one of the Magisters, Motai. Something about it seemed weird but I blew it off trying to keep up with Elora.

I looked at her, floored. "When do we have time for that?"

She frowned. "Now, Commander. The time is always now. All you need to do is get that A.I. assistant of Kirpich's in touch with our Tech Guru."

"Guru?"

Elora laughed. "Your language, Commander, not mine. Our Disana is a singular being. She is more than Zari and less than a machine. Now that the repairs to the ship are nearly completed, she's back in blue sector, bored out of her mind. She needs a challenge."

"Viginti."

Elora nodded. "We had a similar problem millennia ago. The Queen Mother believes there are far too many on the ship already. I have heard rumors that there is discontent among them, too. Stripping them for components could very well create a tipping point. I know you saw her reaction."

I nodded. "She was horrified. And I've heard her speak about being nothing more than a slave. But at the same time, she displayed a haughtiness when I questioned her abilities. I can certainly see how a collective inferiority complex like that could go south."

Elora nodded. "And now is not the time to deal with it."

"I'll bring Viginti to the rec center. She's not going to be damaged, is she?"

"No. Disana will have her scanned, reprogrammed and back up top without a clue."

"Reprogrammed?"

"She'll be the new voice of reason." Elora's expression grew severe. "And the key to shutting them all down, if need be."

I nodded. I couldn't think of doing anything else. The crazy on this ship was piling up. It was wearing on me.

One way or the other, it would all be over soon.

All I had to do was fly my mission and let it take me where it may.

Chapter 15

Insertion into the Anowi system went off without a hitch and, thankfully, without any company.

I already had the pre-flight done on the drop ship and sat with the engines at station strapped in and ready to go.

I was nervous, to be sure. But I wasn't afraid.

The Queen Mother sat with me a long time helping me get my head on straight.

It wasn't easy.

Something still bothered me about their 'adjustments' to Viginti. As much as I loved the Zari, something felt off. I needed to keep an eye on it.

I had to remember who was signing my check.

"We're go for power up, Commander."

Slim's voice seemed deeper through the uplink. It was soothing.

"Copy, powering up."

I powered up my brand-new Zarian command crown and merged with the ship.

Taito's genius new flight interface coupled with the Zarian technology had created a giant leap forward in powered flight.

The ship and I were one.

Slim was our liaison to reality.

"We are go, for launch, Commander. Four minutes until Well activation."

I frowned while running a fast few thousand calculations through my armor's network. Then, eased the dropship from the deck.

"Copy, go. Time to earn our keep."

The superheated plasma swirling inside the maelstrom of the Well's magnetic event horizon was breathtaking. Its palatine rainbow illuminated the emptiness to dance across the broad bow of the ship.

I eased the dropship out across the event horizon to its center hovering briefly before pitching forward ninety degrees to point our nose at the target. I held my breath as the pulsating void opened to the oblivion of hyperspace.

It was a heavy moment.

I toggled my visual display over to the ship's imaging system as I came to a relative stop. Watching the maelstrom helped me adjust to the 360-degree field of vision.

It was a task of complete focus.

"Shaytan Actual, I'm in position. Systems go for launch."

"Confirmed, Commander, you are go for launch."

I smiled. "Slim? You ready to kick some ass?"

"Let's do it."

Then, after a long slow cleansing breath, I launched us into chaos.

I braced myself as the onslaught of energy from luminous tendrils of quanta warped the space out ahead. The ship hit the wave tops with a deep shudder as I began our descent.

We found ourselves fighting for every meter as we met the matter stream head on. There were currents and eddies present that I'd never seen before.

Moving through hyperspace from point to point in the galaxy was a lot like surfing on an ocean. You placed yourself at the crest of a wave and rode it to your destination. In civilized space it was an automated trip as the A.I.'s flew predetermined routes.

Dropping through hyperspace into the Equispance was more akin to diving to the bottom of the ocean in a submarine. There were constant problems of current and pressure changes incurred for every kilometer of descent.

In other words, there was no clear path. One had to fight over, around and through the matter currents to descend.

"Slim, wedge the shields 30 degrees aft by starboard. Reverse to port on my mark."

The shields assisted in navigation as both a sail and rudder in addition to their duty of keeping my ass from being irradiated. I'd ordered it dug in to a dense current to sidestep an eddy rising into view. I tipped the ship in a deep bank using the shield to gather momentum.

"Mark."

As I hoped, the shield helped spin us wildly around the swirl and launched us through a gap in the current.

"Watch your speed, Commander. We're approaching the point of Olankampf's folly."

I nodded, taking a series of deep breaths as I eased up on the throttle. “Damnit, Slim, I wanted it to be a surprise.”

“I was inclined to overlook it until you decided to slingshot us there.”

Suddenly, far below me, I saw a current storm the size of a star system rising into view. I dropped back throttles looking for a current that would lead us away.

“Yeah, let’s not even go there,” Slim reconfigured the display. “I see an alternative rising at three o’clock.”

Slim illuminated the path in my optical matrix. I banked the ship and managed to come in shallow enough to catch its crest. “How far do you think this will take us off course?”

“Who cares? We can reacquire course once we enter the Equispance.”

I didn’t agree but I didn’t see an alternative either. I just had to keep an eye on the lateral distance traveled and look for insertion points close in below the storm.

“Commander, reverse course, come to 30 degrees port.”

I corrected our course and watched as the vortex once again filled my forward vision. "I sure as hell hope you're having an epiphany, Slim."

"I just figured out where Olankampf went wrong."

I rolled the ship around a collapsing pressure wave as the flow of its current destabilized. The ship vibrated around me as we crashed through the wave top.

I bit my lip. "Do tell."

"He tried to go around the vortex too and found himself fighting the current speeds at the edges. That was those last few lateral readings we didn't understand."

I shook my head as I fought to maintain control. The current at the periphery of the vortex crashed against the shields shaking the ship. I heard the hull issue a few furtive squeaks around me. "And we about did the same thing. Great."

"Head for the eye. The current speeds will be slower closer to the center."

I flipped the ship through another void and aimed for the eye of the storm. "No way out but through, I guess."

“Exactly.” Slim quickly dropped composition data on my display. “It should take us straight into the Equispance.”

“If the pressure doesn’t crush us first. Look at those density readings.”

“Once we drop into the eye, we won’t need the shields to maneuver. We’ll pull them in close and hope they hold.”

“That’s not much of a plan.” I struggled to keep the ship centered. “Wedge the shields bow center. I’m going to punch our way in.”

Slim’s precision with the shields pierced the dense gas above the eye. The ship shuddered mightily as we crossed the event horizon. It caused the external imagers to blink like a strobe. I focused my full attention on the telemetry reading as I fought to keep my breakfast down. The hull plates squealed in terrible harmony and for one great loathing second, I didn’t think we were going to make it.

Then, slowly, the ship steadied. As it did a growing luminescence appeared outside. As the imaging cleared, I searched for detail in my surroundings. The light grew quickly blinding. I toggled through shade filters to continue searching when my command crown suddenly blinked out, leaving me in darkness.

“Slim, I’ve lost all my data.”

Silence.

"Slim, I need a telemetry report. Do you copy?"

More silence.

I tapped the thrusters, seeking a reaction from the ship. I couldn't tell if there was power to any of the ship's systems. I had zero information.

We were dead in space.

We may have just been voided and hadn't realized it, yet.

The thought was maddening.

I took another deep breath and felt a coolness in the air. I realized I was still on the ship and the atmosphere was cooling because the systems were down.

I was alive, but probably not for long.

I disengaged my command crown and waited for my eyesight to filter back. As I sat there dazed, at some great distance I couldn't fathom, I heard music.

The eerie pattern of sound complimented the fuzzy plasma flow glowing outside. As my eyesight returned, I became transfixed with the motion of the energy patterns. There were shades of palatinate and magenta flowing through an endless azure that I'd only seen in dreams.

As I sat there immersed in the soft wash of melody, it occurred to me that this place was purgatory, this netherworld nestled between realities, between Universes.

"Hello?"

This was a place where energy sheltered awaiting rebirth. A subtle realm shielded from the chaos surrounding it.... a sanctuary.

There was a hell of a lot more going on here than anyone topside could have guessed.

"I know someone is there. I didn't bring the tunes with me. Who are you?"

The drop in temperature seemed to have leveled off temporarily, or I was already numb.

"So did you do this, or did you just drop by to see the aftermath?"

The music seemed to fade. I must have scared them.

"Don't go away. Shit, grab a seat and hang out. I'd rather not freeze to death by myself."

The twinkling music seemed fainter but was still quite present.

"My name's Nena, by the way. In case you were wondering. I'm Janusian."

The twinkling seemed suddenly louder. It was as if a second entity had joined us.

"Tell your buddy to settle in too. There's plenty of room if we're all just sitting around."

The music maintained an even keel. I didn't know if they could hear me or not, but it made me feel better. If I couldn't find a way to restore power, I only had about an hour's worth of breathable air left in the ship and maybe another two in my armor. The armor couldn't generate an atmosphere long without an external power source.

I hadn't thought to bring one along.

I released my restraints and climbed out of the seat. "You all don't know anything about fusion inverters, do you? Mine appear to be on the fritz."

Nothing. Just the same shimmery drone.

I walked over to Slim's station and found everything dead. I couldn't even tell if the reactor was working. Its system was separate from the rest of the ship and self-powered. They never went out completely.

"Well fellas, it looks like I'm fucked. I can't get a reading on this reactor. That's not good news. Looks like you may be stuck with me for a while. At least until I asphyxiate. You won't want to stick around for that. It'll be ugly."

The drone continued unabated.

"Of course, some people get off on that. I've seen it too many times, unfortunately. This damn war has made it all too common. That bloodlust becomes an addiction. The worst of all. I fell there myself once, a long time ago. It nearly destroyed me."

The droning suddenly became more distinct. It had moved closer.

"How? I'm afraid that's not a pretty story. I come off badly in it."

Again, it sounded louder, closer. Interested?

"Okay. If you insist. Let me preface this thing by saying that I was once a woman madly in love. Back before the war started, I was a knuckleheaded second lieutenant with big boobs and a bigger mouth. I'd just gotten my first combat assignment and was posted on the frontier. I was becoming lethal in my brand spanking new generation five jump bomber. I was wild. I was brazen. I thought I had the world by the ass. That's when I met Jian."

His name incited tears.

"Jian was a civilian. He worked for the planetary news service. He was on base doing a story about an annual charity event that the local admiralty supported. Our meeting was fate. He was being cleared to interview the admiral when I, by total chance, had to stop at administration to clear up a payroll issue. Normally I was never on that side of the base. So, it was just a crazy quirk of circumstances that our eyes met in that corridor. It's a moment I'll never forget."

I stopped. I had to sit down. I dropped on the ledge bordering the cockpit.

The memory was too much. I wasn't sure I wanted to relive it.

I started toggling through the armor's computer to see if it had a heat mode across which I hadn't stumbled. As I sat distracted, the drone grew louder.

I looked toward it. "You really want to hear the rest?"

That time I heard two distinct sets of twinkles. I wasn't alone. And they were interested.

Or I was suffering from hypothermia and hypoxia.

If they were real, I hoped they were inclined to help me out. But first things first.

I took a deep breath and held it trying to get a grip. I exhaled slowly watching the steam flow out before me.

It was time to set it all to rest.

"Jian and I enjoyed an entire idyllic year together. We'd found our balance in the rush of being career-minded individuals. And we were just crazy in love. I adored his every breath. He was one of the most intelligent men I had ever met. And, if you knew anything about my father, you'd know that's a powerful statement. Jian just made me better, more grounded. I was tuned in and involved. I'd been promoted to first lieutenant and given command of a squadron while we were together. He had counseled me in the politics of it. My efforts were quickly noticed. It was the best time of my life."

I smiled into the multi-colored darkness. I could have held that feeling forever.

"On our first anniversary he proposed to me. He had taken me into the capital for dinner and gave me the ring while we were waiting for dessert. He followed the old Earth custom of getting down on one knee. I didn't know what was going on. I'd thought he'd lost his fork!"

"Then, when I figured out what was going on, I started crying like any fresh new spring bride and accepted immediately. The patrons applauded. And we ended up getting our dessert and a bottle of booze for free, a gift from the manager. It was a perfect evening. I was enchanted."

I paused, staring down at the floor. It took a concerted effort for me to vacate that memory for the next. The weight on my heart was as heavy now as it was then.

"Then the war came. The bastard Aratani. Two weeks before we were set to be married the entire frontier was put on alert. We were sent a carrier and put on patrol when the Aratani attacked. Their engagement with the carrier group was a ruse. They drew us out of the system so they could attack the planet directly. The planetary defense was overwhelmed. And we couldn't get to them. We were pinned down.

"They destroyed the base and most of the capital. Including the media tower where Jian worked. I was told he was at his desk when the attack began. He started helping to evacuate the building when it suffered several direct hits from Aratani missiles. There were few survivors."

My tears flowed freely. I could see him there trying his best to help. After all these years it was still heartbreaking.

"We fought the Aratani tooth and nail for a week to give the civilians time to evacuate. We were lucky, most got out. But it decimated the carrier group. My last memory of Zuridan was slicing across the system to get my squadron onto a carrier diverted to pick up survivors. I could see the scars on the planet and the smoke from fires still burning. I screamed inside the cockpit knowing I had to leave Jian behind, that he would never have a proper burial, that we would never have a home together or kids. As I raced away from the planet in tears, my heart shattered. The girl I was died there that day."

The twinkling fell to a muted silence.

"The officer that emerged on Ganivet eight days later was a different creature all together. She was a feral being bent on revenge. I become the angel of death to those that took my Jian from me. I became the Dragon Queen."

The drone chimed inquisitively.

"That's exactly what I did. I unleashed hell. I was fearless. My bloodlust carried me on a tear that lasted decades. I have more certified kills than half of the NMK squads combined. I killed Aratani. That became the whole of my existence."

The droning faded a bit and reached a few new pitches I hadn't heard. It sounded like they were conferring.

"I'm sorry. Am I boring you?"

The droning intensified and drew closer.

"What happened?"

A resounding yes.

"Okay. I got you." I couldn't help giggling. I didn't know if any of this was real or not, but it was a trip.

"The long and the short of it is that my bloodlust ran away with me. After all those years I was still bent, more so. I had grown arrogant, self-righteous and that led to a fatal error."

"My squad and I were part of a mission over Almawty. We had taken the bastards by surprise and were turning their colony into dust. I was returning to base when I saw one of the big Aratani shuttles trying to sneak out. I reported it and the squad, and I headed back out. We were about halfway there when I got a ship-to-ship signal telling me to stand down."

"Who the hell is this?' I didn't have crown confirmation, but I could see a K fighter closing in quickly."

"This is Captain Edsala Cray, commander of the Inferia. Do not pursue."

I looked out toward the drone.

"I'd never heard of the guy, and I was one not to be deterred. 'Sorry Captain, I have my orders. Nothing leaves this system.' I shut down the radio and hit the thrusters. 'Fuck this turkey."

"The next thing I know, this Captain Cray drops in from above firing at me. That's when I lost it. I sent the squad on to take out the transport and went after this Captain Cray. My blood was boiling. I banked around and got behind him quickly. He was fairly skilled, but I was bent. I was on him in a flash."

I stared out at the energy field as I pulled myself together. "I pulled the trigger. On a superior officer. It had always been my contention that I was only trying to disable Cray's ship to keep him from firing on us. But here, now, I must be honest with you boys. I meant to kill the son of a bitch. My bloodlust was firmly in control of me."

"I went to prison for it. The JAG and jury didn't buy my bullshit. I'd broken the Gamma Tenet."

"What was worse was the Admiralty discovered that the transport we destroyed contained only hatchlings, the infirm and elderly. I'd have fired even knowing it, such was the depth of my rage. But it affected my wingman, Meegie, deeply. She took her own life while my trial was going on. That sealed my fate. It was the smack to the face that I needed to realize exactly what I had become. If my parents were alive, they would have been ashamed. And thus, finally, after the anger had completely eaten me up inside, I was ashamed too."

"And now here I am stuck who knows where with a pair of twinkling ghosts still coming up short. This war must end. I don't know if you guys can help or not help or whatever, but I must complete this mission. I don't care anymore if the Aratani live or die. I just want to live in peace."

Then eerily the droning faded.

"Commander Videt, you've disengaged your uplink, why?"

Slim's voice caused me to jump nearly out of my skin. I jerked around to see the ship's systems active and normal around me.

It was warm!

"Well, it's about damn time." I reengaged my crown. "I could have used you a couple of hours ago."

Slim huffed. "What did you mean a couple of hours ago? The interface has the mission in its thirty-first minute."

“Yeah, well the interface is wrong. I’ve been floating down stream here for a few hours.”

“Were you operating out of synch through the Zarian interface? Maybe it was that.”

“I disengaged it when the power went down. I was sitting here staring at the plasma flow, reminiscing for hours. I could feel the atmosphere in the ship getting cold. It was real.”

There was the briefest of pauses. “Your body temperature is well below normal.”

“I told you.”

“It looks like there’s a discrepancy between the ship’s clock and the mission interface.”

“Yeah, that’s not weird or nothing, huh?”

“I agree with you. But I can’t recall a second’s loss. My internal diagnostic notes no anomalies.”

“Well, Slim, old buddy, looks like we have ourselves an enigma.”

“It’s the gifts you don’t know about that really stick with you.”

“Indeed.”

I retook control of the ship and pushed it forward. The Equispance was a lot more subdued than the layers above it. You still had to keep an eye out for a passing matter stream or plasma discharge. It wasn't a gimmie.

"I'm going to try to establish a secondary link and see if we can account for this discrepancy."

I gazed out as the familiar haze shimmered around me. "Triangulate how far off course we are, too."

"As ordered."

Judging by his tone, I guessed Slim was questioning whether we were both in our right minds or not.

I wasn't sure myself.

"Commander, I have us on course at a distance of one thousand and fifty-eight A.U."

I nodded absently still trying to account for the expansion of time.

"Commander?"

"Well, hot damn, I guess we made it. That makes me feel better."

"I have the Antithesian beacon on-line. Docking procedure will commence in ten minutes standard."

I felt better knowing Slim didn't dismiss my story outright. He was still an A.I., though. He wouldn't be convinced until the data had been processed and cross referenced.

As I sat waiting for the docking sequence to commence, I heard music, once again, creep into my head. It felt stronger this time, more immediate. It wasn't like the entities I'd dealt with earlier. This one felt dangerous.

Bottom line, I didn't feel safe. This entity was powerful. Like we could be shrugged off into quanta as a mere nuisance.

The thought made me shudder.

For a few harrowing minutes it wandered the ship around me. It mostly just seemed curious. There didn't seem to be a point in contacting Slim. If it didn't register on the ship's sensors, he'd think I was really losing it.

So, I just sat studying the descent data and let it do its thing, while holding my breath and trying to remain silent.

I'd heard that this was what it was like to be in the presence of one of the ancient races. From what I know of them some could have easily made a home here. I just doubted very much that they'd be willing to share territory.

That's why they were scoping us out.

"Transfer has commenced, Commander. Count-down to launch in twenty-two minutes."

"Copy. Systems at station. Countdown set at twenty-two minutes. Mark"

The entity disappeared at the sound of Slim's voice. They were more skittish than I thought. Or they were content that we weren't staying. Who knows?

It was the longest twenty-two minutes of my damned life. And I'd done time.

The experience had me frazzled.

I needed to get out of here.

Chapter 16

Kirpich stalked the room as the department heads rushed around him to set up shop in the Tech Corp conference room. Taito, Lam and Nalwist led teams at different stations pouring over the drop-ship's data. Slim's hologram stood beside me, having been downloaded to join the debriefing.

I was getting used to him. He'd proven his meddle.

It was a miracle we made it back to the Shaytan. The flight out was as harrowing as our descent only without the crazy light show. My perception of time was spot on, however. We had lost three hours in-bound.

We were gone so long that the crew had just about given up on our return.

They damn near powered down the Well.

Kirpich stopped behind Nalwist to glance at his screens. Nalwist did a double take, big eyes agog, and sped up his process.

"So, what do we know? What happened out there?"

Everyone glanced around and murmured but no one wanted to speak up.

It was much too early to tell. Post-mission takes hours on a routine flight, let alone this debacle.

"I know I've never had a drop go like that." I captured Kirpich's attention, taking the onus off the crowd. "And this is my tenth drop, so I'm a bit of an expert."

"So run through it again for me, Commander."

Kirpich took a seat back at the table. "When did you lose power?"

The techs behind him looked visibly relieved.

Nalwist breathed a sigh of relief.

"As soon as we entered the eye. I was checking the pressure on the shields when everything went black."

"And you continued to descend."

I nodded emphatically. "Through the craziest cosmic kaleidoscope of colors ever conceived. I was mesmerized. After a good while sitting there freezing my ass off and talking to myself, I decided it wasn't the worst way to go. But it was still going to suck."

Kirpich scowled at the fast fit of giggles but didn't say anything.

"And then everything just came back."

"Like it hadn't stopped. Slim was monitoring our descent. The ship was listing a bit while I was off evincing. When he spoke, I nearly jumped out of my skin."

Kirpich looked at Slim. "What did it look like to you?"

"I just thought she was daydreaming. I had no indication otherwise."

"What was your first clue something was off?"

"After the commander confided her experience, I checked the quantum clock and found a discrepancy. But, given the nature of the mission, I wanted to compare it to a clock here first to rule out irradiation."

"The three hours just kind of stuck out on its own." I crossed my arms and slid down in my chair.

"Mightily," Kirpich nodded.

"The commander's body temperature also showed evidence of exposure to cold. When I scanned her it was at thirty-five point nine."

"Hyperthermic?" The admiral turned to me.

"For real." I nodded. "It was a cold mother-fucker, sir."

"What did you do during this time?"

I hesitated. I wasn't about to divulge my ghost story. They already thought I was nuts.

"Pretty much bitched about freezing my ass off. But I did save room for a little introspection."

That was close enough.

Kirpich turned to Nalwist. "How in the hell do you account for that?"

"I can't." Nalwist shrugged. "Our initial analysis on the dropship shows no anomalies."

"Except for the clock." Slim walked over to observe Nalwist's screen.

As the conversation livened, Elora came in with Bootah in tow. The girl looked relieved when she saw me.

It was sweet.

Elora caught my eye and nodded. She looked proud.

"To be honest, sir, I'm not sure I could pull that off again." I looked him dead in the eye. "We're lucky we made it out of there at all."

"I understand your concerns, Commander, but we can scarcely afford to deviate from the schedule. Now that you know what to expect, you'll be better prepared for your next drop."

I glanced at Slim, shaking my head in frustration.

"Admiral, with all due respect, this is a troubling phenomenon. This time dilation could very well jeopardize the mission. It was only a matter of a few hours this time. What if that changes? We could get stuck there for days or months, or permanently. Hell, Olankampf could still be in there. He may still fly out of that thing."

Kirpich took umbrage but, to my great relief, let it pass. He dropped into a chair and didn't speak. He started rubbing his temples, his eyes cast to the table.

"Nalwist, what's your take on all this?"

Nalwist turned from his screen, flustered as usual. "Commander Videt raises a valid argument,

Admiral. The interval of her disappearance may well have been nothing more than a quirk of her entry point into the eye. Time may be as much in flux there as is the energy field.

Kirpich frowned. He understood the implication. But his primary concern was procuring the hyper-matter. "We have to forge ahead."

He rose from his chair to resume pacing. "I know it raises the stakes greatly, Commander. But I need at least one more load. If you do this, I will uphold our bargain."

All I could do was nod. If there was a chance of getting another load out, I had to take it.

It was about a whole hell of a lot more than just me.

"When do we launch, sir?"

Kirpich nodded his approval, "Tomorrow, O six hundred. No matter what happens, Commander, we vacate this system at noon. Make sure you don't doddle."

"Well, maybe we'll get lucky and Olankampf will find his way out, too."

Kirpich, at long last, grinned. "Well, if he does, he damn sure better be loaded."

"Commander, did you pick up any scanning signals while you were awaiting transfer?" Nalwist looked my way.

I glanced at Slim. "No. We didn't have any kind of alarm. Why?"

"There is evidence of a most unusual radiation signature emanating from the deck. I've not seen anything like it."

Ah! My visitor in the cockpit left a little something behind. That was interesting.

Nalwist could track that whole mess down with his science kit.

"Is it catalogued?" Kirpich asked.

"Cross referencing now, sir." Nalwist tapped quickly on his display.

Gevin came into the room accompanied by Dr. Gilomi. In that strange second, they made a very handsome couple.

I wondered if they were.

Gevin came straight to me with a quick embrace. The relief in his eyes was genuine.

And touching.

"By the stars, woman. Will you ever cease trying to scare the hell out of me?"

"What fun would that be?"

Dr. Gilomi touched my shoulder. "Glad to have you back, Commander. Well done."

"Thank you, ma'am."

"What have we learned?" Gevin asked.

"Not a lot, yet. Nothing to explain the time loss. Nalwist found traces of some weird unknown radiation inside the cockpit."

"Really? Interesting." Dr. Gilomi turned to Gevin. "I think I'll have a look."

Gevin smiled. "I'm sure Commander Nalwist would appreciate the help."

His eyes followed her as she crossed the room.

There it was. They were a couple. Or they were sure as hell playing at it.

I was glad he was happy. It wasn't an easy find.

I noticed Elora moving to join us after setting Bootah to guard the door.

"Commander, it's good to see you in one piece."

I grinned, wrapping Elora in a hug. "It's good to be in one piece."

"Captain, I hope you'll forgive the intrusion. Bootah and I are both of the type to have to see with our own eyes what others can accept audibly. We had to see that the commander was safe ourselves."

Gevin smiled. "No intrusion at all, ma'am. We sent word of the meeting in case the Queen Mother wished to attend."

"Thank you, Captain. I am happy to stand in her stead. She is involved in a bit of research right now. Of all her strengths it is her insatiable curiosity that overarches. After this incident with the commander, she decided to see if there was anything in our records about hyperspace that might be of use."

"Ah, that is most welcome, Elora. Thank her for me," Gevin smiled.

"Me too." I grinned.

Elora touched my arm. "We are committed to keeping you safe, Nena Videt. No Zari walks alone."

I smiled, misty again.

When did I turn into such a crybaby?

"Thanks, Elora."

"As soon as you are able, the Queen Mother wishes you to attend. Hopefully, she will have something of use."

"I'll get there as quickly as I can." I smirked. "This data dump may take a while."

"Well, at least come to evening repast. You're welcome too, Captain."

"Thank you, Elora. I just may take you up on that." Gevin smiled graciously.

Elora's smile was alluring. "We'd be happy to have you."

Wow. No masked intentions there.

Gevin looked the tiniest bit frightened.

"I hope to see you both this evening," Elora walked to the door to stop beside Bootah. "Stay with the commander."

Bootah's smile shone like a supernova. "Thank you, ma'am."

Great.

Elora glanced at me and winked. "Soon."

Something was afoot. Elora was playing something close to the vest.

We worked for the better part of eight hours to arrive at the dazzling conclusion that we had absolutely no idea what caused the loss of time.

By the time we reached that conclusion it was more than a little galling.

We had gone through the data from start to finish, every zero and every damn one and the only things in the dropship that experienced the true passage of time were me and the cesium in the ship's clock. Everything else moved forward at a decimal thereof. By our best estimate, from Slim's perspective, I'd only lost about twenty seconds.

Daydreaming.

The clincher on the weirdness factor was the metallurgical analysis on the dropship's hull. All the carbonalium and ferrite on the ships outer plating decayed at the abbreviated rate. Yet, the clock ticked on.

"The physicists back at Fleet would have a field day with this." Taito deactivated his screen in frustration.

"They'd probably say we'd lost our damn minds."

"Ah, but we have the data to back it up, Commander." Nalwist rose from his seat to stretch. "This divergence is a fact. I suspect it will be fodder for a spirited debate."

"I'm afraid that won't be possible." Kirpich sat up, suddenly cognizant from his place at the table. "All records from this mission are to be classified and held in thrall for several decades at least."

Nalwist looked genuinely disappointed. I almost felt sorry for the little clucker.

"Well, be that as it may, none of this is going to help Slim and I on our next go around, so with your permission, Admiral, I'm going to call it a day. The girls have supper waiting."

I glanced at Bootah and winked. Her big bright grin returned. To her credit, she had stood her post the entire shift and not spoken a word.

"Granted," Kirpich nodded. "Let's all call it a day. We've gleaned all we can from this data. We will reconvene at O four-thirty for pre-launch tomorrow. Dismissed."

The crowd quickly stowed their gear and prepared to shuffle out. I grabbed Bootah and skipped out ahead stretching my legs in a power walk. Bootah scooted to stay beside me as I crossed the deck for the local lift.

"I take it your meeting did not go well?"

I sighed. "Nowhere is more accurate."

"They don't know what happened to you?"

"They do not, my dear, and neither do I. And I still have another mission to fly."

"We were worried when you didn't return on time," Bootah's face grew sad. "The Queen Mother was most anxious. She is really taken with you, Commander. As am I."

I grinned. "Thank you, Bootah. You all have been a gift to me, too. I am grateful to walk among you."

Bootah smiled. "It is an honor to walk beside you."

I rested my hand on her shoulder, grinning, as we stepped into the lift.

It was best feeling in the cosmos to know they truly cared.

Chapter 17

The Queen Mother had me and my evening meal brought to her quarters. She and Elora were sitting at the formal table having a lively discussion with a data pad sitting on the table between them.

The Queen Mother was tapping it rigorously and saying something emphatic in her native language. She quickly cut it off as I came in. She and Elora exchanged glances as they stood to greet me.

Something was up. I just didn't know if I had the heart to find out what it was.

"Commander, we were just discussing you. Please, sit down and join us."

That put me even more ill at ease. I was burnt on bad news. "Thank you?"

I watched as they regarded each other. There was a whole non-verbal conversation going on to which I wasn't privy. Gevin and I had our own silent shorthand. I could only imagine how it would be of sisters.

I'd often thought it would have been nice to have one.

"Elora and I are overjoyed that you made it back safely. You had us worried for a minute, young lady."

"Yeah, I wasn't digging it, either." I smirked, looking my dinner over. "Thanks, though, I appreciate your concern. But I knew going in it was far from being a lock."

The Queen Mother nodded. "Elora told me about the time discrepancy. It must have been maddening just sitting there."

I looked at the Queen Mother and lifted an eyebrow. "It might have been if I was alone."

Surprise registered on their faces.

"Who was there?" Elora asked.

I took a quick bite of Torka bread then flushed it with mead. "As best I could tell there were three separate entities. Two seemed like children. I told them a story to pass the time."

The Queen Mother shot Elora a knowing look.

"The third was decidedly not a child. It was powerful." I looked at both in turn. "It was flipping scary. Also, it didn't appear until after time had been restored. It seemed like it was cleaning up a mess the children made."

"Interesting." The Queen Mother paced the room. "But I fear your meeting may be much more significant than that."

I sighed, like there wasn't enough going on already. "Aren't you full of good news."

The Queen Mother's smile was reticent.

"While you were missing, I started digging into our database about hyperspace anomalies and deep point jumping. Most civilized societies have the good sense not to do so, but there are exceptions. One that was noted in our records was a race called the Mahj. They were extinct millenia before the Zari were conceived. They were traders, like the Union. But they had developed the ability to jump to the opposition quadrants to do business."

"You know, I'd thought that possible. I wrote a paper on it at the academy. My stellar navigation instructor liked the theory but said it was impossible."

The Queen Mother grinned. "Did you get a bad mark?"

"Pissed me straight off." I grinned. "I had the courses plotted. No one had balls enough to try it. Or so I'd thought."

"Well, the Mahj did it for millenia. They're the reason we know anything about life on the other side of the galaxy. Once I started digging, I found something extraordinary in their records."

"Course charts?" I ventured.

"A very disturbing legend."

Groovy.

I looked at Elora. She shrugged. "I was inclined to dismiss it until you brought up your company."

"You two aren't doing a thing to make me feel better."

The Queen Mother's expression softened. "I'm sorry, child, but I didn't want to keep this hidden from you."

I smiled. "I appreciate it, Great Mother."

"Why didn't you tell your superiors about this phenomenon?" Elora looked at me.

"Well, for one, I didn't want them to think I was losing it. And two, Nalwist found evidence of them in the form of some exotic radiation. So, they're on the case. I just figured it would be an unneeded distraction."

Elora seemed satisfied with the answer.

"I'm happy you confided it in us." The Queen Mother smiled. "It is a sign of trust I do not take lightly."

"Thank you, Great Mother."

"So, anyway, to the legend. Let me preface this by saying that Union contact and cooperation with these Antithessians has been troubling for us. We understand the need. We are just of the mind that your board of directors went into this thing blind. Willfully so. After my reading today I find it even more troubling."

Elora looked on impatiently but didn't speak.

"The Mahj spoke of an ancient time when beings from another dimension tried to destroy the galaxy. The legend goes that if left unchecked their technology could negate our entire galaxy as fuel to power their own. This deal with the Antithessians sounds like an inroad to the same thing."

"I understand the concept," I said, "but I think I'm missing the path."

"Think about it." The Queen Mother turned to face us. "Somehow, from the depths of whatever ruddy existence they dwell in, they just happen to contact a civilization on this side that just happens to be mired in a bloody, protracted, war and quickly growing desperate. Then they offer help, an ineffable power source to turn the tide. Why?"

Elora and I exchanged glances. It was a very good question.

"To do what we're about to. Unleash a new age of warfare in the galaxy. The ability to destroy entire star systems, entire civilizations. We stand on the verge of being able to negate our own existence. And as we stagger along that path, these Anthessians feed us our death until there's nothing left. Then, they jump in and finish it off. All they'll have to do is knock over a corpse. Then, they can turn the whole bloody mess into a fuel depot."

The thought was wholly unsettling.

"So does the legend say what happened?" I paused to refill my mug with mead. "How were they stopped?"

"The legend says their attack was thwarted by a powerful ancient race called the Logion. It is written that they had a massive spacefaring empire when the Kah'lah and Mitori were still drawing pictographs in caves."

"Wow. That's old."

The Queen Mother giggled. "Precisely. After the invasion was repelled, the Logion placed guardians at the midpoint between our galaxy and theirs to keep the two sides from ever having contact again."

"And you think that's who I was just hanging out with?"

The Queen Mother nodded sternly. "I do."

I didn't know how to react. Part of me just wanted to scream like a baby and run into my mother's arms. The other parts of me agreed.

I just could not win for losing.

I wanted to scream but I couldn't lose my composure in front of the Queen Mother. I rested my hand on my forehead, hiding my eyes, as I took a few deep breaths trying to maintain my composure.

It wasn't easy.

"So, if these guardians didn't know what was up before, they do now."

The Queen Mother nodded, rising from her seat to come sit next to me. "I fear it so."

I laughed to keep from crying. "So why didn't they do anything about it?"

"I was wondering that myself." Elora gazed at the Queen Mother.

"Who knows? They may be studying the problem. It would be to our advantage if they were over contemplative. Or I could very well be wrong. The stories about the Logion could be only legends. I just find the coincidences concerning. We can ill afford to be lax on any detail at this juncture."

Her last statement hung heavy in the air.

"So, nothing changes." I smirked before taking a very long drink of mead.

"I make the drop tomorrow and roll the bones."

"Forewarned is forearmed." The Queen Mother stopped behind me to squeeze my shoulders. "You will just have to consider it another variable in the equation."

In that moment it didn't feel like a cold calculation. It felt like doom.

My doom.

I hoped she was wrong.

Chapter 18

My fitful attempt at sleep was cut woefully short by the blaring klaxon of a security alert. I pulled my pillow around my ears to shut it out. Short of the ship blowing apart, I didn't give a damn what was going on.

My nerves were fraying. I needed sleep.

But then my armor jingled. I whined and kicked the bed a few times before activating my command crown.

"Good morning, Elora."

Elora evoked a hopeful grin. "I know. I'm sorry, child."

"What's the problem?"

I was beyond incredulous.

"A faction of hybrids has taken control of main propulsion. They killed the systems chief and are holding his staff hostage."

The Alazai, Major Pava. The one that wanted to pluck Nalwist for skirting regs.

Damn. I liked that guy.

"What do you want me to do?" I asked, not entirely pleasant.

Elora raised an eyebrow. "Find out why they butchered Viginti before seizing the powerplant."

I sat up in bed. "Butchered? No shit?"

"I'm afraid not, my dear. They ripped her processing unit from her open skull."

"Damn, that's rough."

"Indeed. I'm confident they can't replicate our technology. But I have no doubt they've already figured out where it came from."

I rose from the bed transforming the nanites from fuzzy pink pajamas to proper armor. As I did, another push chime came through. Gevin.

"I got to go, Elora. Captain, online."

"Keep me apprised."

I clicked over as I headed for the hatch. "Ready for duty, Captain."

Gevin's eye roll made me giggle. "Meet me on the propulsion deck. I've got a job for you."

"Okay."

"Be careful on your way back. I've given orders to shut all the hybrids down. There's been a bit of resistance."

I recognized that droll tone. It was a total bleeding damn mess. But not worth losing one's dignity over. The man was a true Mariner.

"Don't worry about me, love. I'm a wrecking ball made of razors."

"That's what I'm talking about. Don't tear up my ship getting back here. They're hybrids, Videt, not Aratani."

I widened my eyes in feigned surprise. "Well damn, Gevin, you just take all the fun out of everything. I'm still trying to learn how to use this rig."

Gevin smirked. "Well let's work on exercising a bit of finesse, shall we? We've quite enough to deal with."

I grinned. "That's why you're the captain."

Another eye roll. He cracked me up.

"Just get here as quick as you can."

"On my way, sir."

I barely made it to the inner hull before I ran into a firefight. Two hybrids in flight crew jumpers were armed with plasma rifles and had three NPs trapped in a dead-end hallway. The NPs were giving them hell but couldn't better their position.

I sped up, running up the wall. The duo turned and started firing at the sound of my charge. I dropped down in a spin, severing their heads with a scythe blade fashioned from my right gauntlet. I'm not sure Gevin would have approved but it was succinct.

The NPs didn't look particularly thrilled about me saving their asses.

"Are you alright?"

The ranking officer, a burly human Lieutenant Commander named Rueben, strode into the main passageway looking over the dead hybrids. "For now, I suppose. But there's a hell of a lot more of them to put down, if they don't blow up the damn ship first."

"Yeah, that would suck." I looked the chubby guy over. "But I think it more likely that we'll hear demands for recognition of hybrid sentience or some such shit."

Rueben shook his head in derision. He paused to spit on the head of one of the fallen. "Like anyone gives a shit."

"Well, the longer they talk the more time we'll have to figure out a way to shut them all down."

Rueben grimaced. "Tell them to hurry up with that shit. I'm losing troops by the second."

I smiled, but I found the man utterly disgusting. "I'll deliver your message to the captain personally. I'm heading for him now."

I captured an image of his fat face. He looked like he swallowed his tongue.

I winked before calling my helmet around my head and raced away.

Gevin was going to love this picture.

The ante deck outside main propulsion was a mob scene of NPs, marines, and techs. Gevin was at the center of the crowd fielding questions. He looked exhausted.

His demeanor was one of absolute calm though as he navigated the barrage of assessments and requests. But I could see anger smoldering deep in his eyes.

They'd messed with his ship and his crew.

This wouldn't stand.

"No. We will hold this position for now. They have the hatchways to the inner deck rigged with I.E.D.s and who knows what else. I want to know what they're looking to accomplish. But I want information and options first. Then we can craft a response."

Gevin looked up and saw me at the back of the crowd. He didn't look enthused. I didn't know what his problem was, but I'd messed up somewhere.

As I made my way through the crowd, I spied Gunny Tropa and his goon squad standing against a bulkhead looking morose. His sudden scowl let me know he'd spotted me, too.

"Why the fuck is she here?"

Lt. Colonel Jai turned and said something I couldn't make out. Whatever it was, the look on Tropa's face was priceless.

I grinned, stopping at the edge of the crowd. I stayed out of the way as Gevin got everyone on task.

Gevin turned his gaze on me as the crowd dispersed. He had a cool tight-lipped expression I knew wasn't good. "Walk with me, Commander."

I kept my mouth shut as we exited the ante hall to the main passageway. We were a few hundred meters down the line before he finally turned to look at me.

"What did the Zari do to Viginti?"

The question took me by surprise. I tried not to let it register on my face.

"I'm not completely sure." It was close enough to the truth. "I know they were afraid of a mutiny among them. They wanted to use her as a calming influence."

Gevin's face reddened. "That's worked out bloody fucking well, hasn't it?"

I'd never seen Gevin lose his temper before. It wasn't pretty.

"Had you not noticed, Gevin? Seriously? I got a sense of it the first time I talked to her. Those creatures are haunted by their own existence. They're a slave species in all but name. And you and the Admiral just keep plugging them in and twisting them to whatever shit task that pops up."

Gevin was taken aback but didn't say anything. I knew he already felt guilty.

"Did you see her in the meeting where you two decided to gut them to power the drones? She was horrified. I saw it. So did the Queen Mother. She was afraid that it would be the turning point. She made the decision to do something about it. I thought she had made her concerns known to the Admiral."

"She did not." Gevin's sense of calm was slowly returning. "She took this upon herself and manipulated you into helping."

"She didn't manipulate shit. You and the Admiral have been so focused on your mission that you can't see what's been going on around you. The hybrids aren't the only ones that are ready to take this tug over. Tropa and his dipshit Marines have a hard-on for the Admiral too. I'm surprised they didn't try to pull some shit when this whole thing jumped off."

Gevin's face paled. He turned away to stare at the floor. I didn't mean to hurt him, but he was in desperate need of a wake-up call.

"You think I've been remiss, Nena?"

His voice wasn't much more than a whisper. He sounded as if his fire had abandoned him.

"I don't know, Gevin. You tell me. I know we need to do something extraordinary to ensure our survival, but this crew is beat. They know how long the odds have grown."

Gevin shook his head. He leaned against the bulkhead and wiped the sweat from his brow. "I know. I've known it since we started pulling together this crew. But there's no alternative. There's no safe harbor. We must see this through."

Gevin turned to look at me. "You know me, Nena. I didn't come to this decision lightly. But after thirty years of slaughter what other choice do we have? They have no respect for any life other than their own. They want to wipe all of us out."

I moved to his side and wrapped my arms around him resting my head on his shoulder. "I think our collective desperation has bred a terrible despair. Logic doesn't thrive in that environment."

I felt Gevin's head lean against mine. He needed the connection as much as I did.

"When did you become so philosophic?"

"A decade in stir will do that to you, if you have the good sense to be open to it."

"You've changed. I could see it in your eyes when we met in the mess hall. The rage was gone. It made me regret dragging you into this."

"Better to die fighting than live on one's knees, I suppose. I worked hard learning to let my rage go. It cost me everything. I had to let it go."

"Well, I'm glad you're here, even if it is a big fucked up mess."

I started giggling like mad. Gevin never, ever, dropped the F bomb.

"I'm glad I got to see you again, no matter what happens. You're the only friend I've got."

Gevin grinned. "Damn. You're in bad shape, lady."

We both started laughing. We were so tired we were slap happy. But it was great to be able to share a quiet moment with him. We stood there for a long time just enjoying the silence.

"So, what's our next move, Captain?"

"My next move is to open negotiations with the hybrids holed up in propulsion. And while I have them distracted; I want you to get the Zari to take them out. They helped create the mess. They can clean it up."

"I don't think that will be a problem. They're already working on that contingency."

Gevin nodded. He seemed resigned to the task. "Like it or not, it seems genocide is the order of the day."

I took my head off his shoulder and hugged him. "This isn't genocide. It's mutiny. We can space every damn one of them."

Gevin issued a thin smile. "Thank you, Nena."

"You're welcome. And, when this is over, I want to get you and the Queen Mother together. She's stumbled across a bit of galactic history I think you and the Admiral should be aware of."

Gevin lifted an eyebrow. "History? Really? With everything else that's going on?"

I nodded, turning to look him in the eye. "She's discovered ancient references to the Antithessians."

"I take it that's not good."

"Not really."

Gevin sighed. He turned away to gaze back up the passageway from where we came. "Let's just focus on one crisis at a time. I'm way too damn tired right now to double up."

I reached over and touched his cheek.

I couldn't begin to imagine the weight of responsibility lying on his shoulders or the pressure he put on himself. Most beings would have already lost it.

"Noted." I broke out into my most charming grin. "And, really, I wouldn't worry about it too terribly much. We'll all be long dead before it becomes an issue."

That got a smile out of him.

"You know full well, Nena Videt, that our luck is never that good."

"Yeah, you're right. But a girl can always hope."

Gevin squeezed my hand before turning to walk away. "You keep right on hoping. One of these days it will actually work. Keep me updated."

"On the hour, sir."

I called my helmet to form and made tracks for blue sector. It was going to be a long day.

Chapter 19

The Queen Mother had Nashumi's platoon assembled and ready to move out by the time I arrived. Their tech 'guru' Disana was with them addressing the troops.

She was a freaky creature. She was so thin and frail that her armor sustained her and kept her moving. She reminded me of my dear friend Magister Lopast. Both gave off a heavy vibe despite their frailty.

"I have downloaded a short burst e-mag pulse weapon to your armor's programming. It will short circuit the hybrids' central processing nexus. You must be within five meters for the signal to be fully effective so be prepared to utilize secondary measures."

The Queen Mother stepped forward. "Nashumi has your assignments. I want this ship to be cleared bow to stern no matter how long it takes. Am I clear?"

"Yes, Queen Mother!"

The Queen Mother grinned. "So, hurry up or you'll miss breakfast."

Nashumi smiled before starting the song that set her troops to move out. Their ease in the face of battle was astonishing.

Elora gathered me in a hug as did the Queen Mother.

"I don't know how you're even on your feet, child. You look exhausted." The Queen Mother held me up.

I glanced at Elora. "Apparently, I'm the go to person to call whenever shit goes wonky on this damned boat. And I'm not even on the command staff."

The Queen Mother giggled before turning her attention to Elora. "Why did you wake her?"

"I set her to discover the motive behind the planted hybrid's disassembly. She knows the ship and customs much better than I."

The Queen Mother scowled. "Is that not apparent? Disana's alterations were discovered."

Disana, who was lost in her own world up until that point, whipped her head around. "That's not possible. My programming was subtle. There's no way it could have been detected."

I frowned. “Didn’t you tell me, Elora, that part of the programming was aimed at altering Viginti’s attitude toward a more passive approach to their dilemma?”

“It was,” Elora confirmed.

“That may well have been the cause. We don’t know to what degree she was involved but I’d say, being as close to the Admiral as she was, she was probably up to her neck in this plot whether she wanted to be or not. A sudden new attitude toward acquiescence may well have been enough to make her a target. But the way she was killed doesn’t really bear that out.”

Disana’s displeasure was on full display.

“My thoughts exactly.” The Queen Mother glared at Disana.

Disana opened her mouth to speak then suddenly thought better of it. She held her gaze on me.

“It may well be that these new hybrids are a lot smarter than we thought.” Elora shifted on her feet. “We may have underestimated them as well.”

“We won’t have to worry long.” Disana turned her gaze to the Queen Mother.” The pulse weapon will make short work of them. Then, we can study the phenomenon in depth.”

The Queen Mother didn't seem taken with Disana's statement. She probably freaked the Queen Mother out, too.

"Well, however it goes down, I'm going back to propulsion. They're working on a way to breach so we can take them down and free the hostages. Is the pulse weapon on my system too, Disana?"

"It is."

I smiled at her. "Excellent! I'm going to volunteer to sneak in and take them out. I don't want Tropa and his jugheads blowing up the ship going in with guns blazing."

The Queen Mother smiled. "Good idea. If you need back-up coordinate with Nashumi. I'll give her a heads up."

"Thank you, Great Mother."

Her smile was warm. "Take good care, my child. These creatures may have tricks they haven't shown yet."

I nodded. "I'll keep that in mind."

Nashumi and the girls were taking hybrids out with extreme prejudice as I made my way back to propulsion. As I crossed into the inner hull, I could see rolling fire fights above me and all down along the inner superstructure.

The girls were popping them with the pulse weapon in mad fashion. I saw several falls over the rails into the central void, soon to be bloody smears on the launch bay doors.

I wouldn't want to draw duty to clean that mess up.

"How many hybrids are onboard?"

My heads-up flashed. *"7,743 in service for current mission."*

"Damn." This was going to take a while. "Have any surrendered to custody?"

"Negative."

I shuddered. Hybrids. Mutineers. Whatever. It was an unprecedented slaughter.

The truth of our terrible fate.

I pulled myself together and decided to take the shortcut up to the higher decks, so I transformed the armor into the four-legged prowler I learned from Nashumi and bolted.

As I raced upward at breakneck speed, I got a push from Taito. My heart sank into my squirming guts as soon as I saw it. Something was wrong.

"Tell me good news, Lieutenant."

"I'll tell you anything you want after you get me the hell out of here. We're being overrun. They killed Nalwist and Lam's in bad shape too. Me and the kid are holding the high ground, but I don't know for how long."

Shit. Shit. Shit. Shit. Shit. Shit. Shit.

"On my way."

I bolted before I had time to think. I was only a few decks below but about five blocks aft. This was going to take a minute. I sprinted up the last few decks and dashed fore. As I did, I pushed Elora and Gevin.

"Yes, child?"

"Nena?"

"I need reinforcements on the Engineering deck A.S.A.F.P. Nalwist is down, and Lam is critical. Taito's holding the office deck for now. I think they're trying to steal tech to escape."

Elora nodded curtly. "On their way, child."

She dropped the link.

"Marines inbound." Gevin replied. "They're trying to access the flight bay on the outer hull. Scrambling fighters too."

"I'm on my way. Will report."

"Happy hunting."

"Copy."

I poured it on for engineering. I don't know if the armor responded to desperation, but I was moving a great clip faster than I had ever gone before. It dawned on me that the limitations of the armor were only manifestations of the limits of one's mind.

I had to learn to push beyond my frailties.

I came at engineering from above slipping in through the ventilation system. The hybrids had Taito and the kid pinned in but weren't advancing on them. They just wanted them out of the way.

The bulk of the group were working to get a larger jump shuttle operational while others attempted to hack the launch doors. It didn't look like either group was having much success.

"I thought you were going to have this ship ready for launch, Ashron."

I risked a peak to see the Simjanian that I met working here.

"I couldn't get all my parts fabricated after the ship was damaged. All the resources were going to repairs." Ashron scowled. "I had to pull what I needed from another ship. Now I'm forced to rig it to make it work. So shut up and let me do it."

As I crossed around to get a better look, I discovered Ashron wasn't talking to another hybrid. He was talking to a Marine.

Enu, one of Tropa's catamites. I started imaging and sent an emergency push straight to Gevin.

Before I could say anything, all hell broke loose.

The huntresses appeared out of nowhere.

They dropped thirty in a coordinated maneuver as soon as they appeared. Ashron fell dead sliding over the side of the craft as Enu dropped to open fire.

I launched from my hiding place and made straight for the traitorous bastard.

He didn't notice my descent. A huntress had him pinned down with a good old-fashioned slug thrower. I saluted her as I dropped on top of him, camera rolling.

"Lance Corporal, you are under arrest for mutiny."

"Fuck you, convict. You're about to die. Worry about that."

I wanted to run a knuckle-spike through his bulbous forehead but refrained. I wanted Gevin to see just how far down the rabbit hole we've gone.

"Who's running this operation? Tropa?"

Enu snorted a laugh. "Tropa, really? I mean you've met him, right?"

I smirked. "Yeah, you got me there. So, what the fuck? Why?"

Enu glared at me, incredulous. "We're tired of dying for these bastards! The Union's done. This whole sector is fucked. It's time to cut our losses and move on to the central systems with the rest of the cast-offs and try to carve out some kind of peace."

It didn't sound like a bad idea. But it was disheartening.

"Stand down. All troops stand down. I am calling for a cessation of hostilities on all sides."

Gevin's announcement rattled through the ship. You could slowly feel the overall vibe mellow.

The ship was quiet. Chaos had temporarily been abated.

His quick flip left me guessing. Why stop?

I stood gauging the room as everyone else looked around staring at each other. I leapt back up to the command tower leaving Enu with the huntresses to ponder his mistakes.

I shoved aside the damaged hatch to look for Taito. As I did, Elora landed on the deck beside. We eased into the room surveying the damage. It was destroyed. Nalwist was lying just inside the door in a heap. He hadn't stood a chance. He'd been shot at least five times. His puffy little frame looked so thin.

I hadn't been crazy about him, but he deserved better than this.

We lit spotlights on our helmets as we moved deeper in the room. We found a blood trail moving back toward the door to the kitchenette. Taito and the kid must have dragged Lam with them inside. I tapped on the door.

"Taito? Are you okay? It's Nena. I have Elora with me."

After a few long seconds, the door slid aside. Ensign Raibous stood staring up at me in shock. He was covered in human blood. Uchawii bled a bizarre hue of baby blue, so he didn't appear to be injured.

"Are you okay, Ensign? Where's Lieutenant Taito?"

Raibous nodded, tears falling from his silver eyes. He pointed to the back of the room but couldn't speak. I wrapped my arm around his shoulder and pulled him close.

Elora found the switch for the lights and illuminated the room. When she did Raibous pushed his face tighter into my shoulder. He didn't want to see what was looming behind him.

I wish I hadn't either.

Taito was sitting on the floor with his back against a counter. He had Lam's body across his lap with his head against his shoulder. When Taito looked up at me my heart broke. The profound sense of pain, confusion and loss present in his eyes was more than I could bear. Lam had died in his arms stuck here in the dark.

I turned to look at Elora for support. Tears rolled down her face as well. I passed Raibous over to her and moved closer to Taito.

"Taito, buddy, are you injured?"

He shook his head, slowly, his arms still wrapped around Lam's body. Lam was covered head to toe in blood. As I got closer, I saw that among his various wounds, he'd been shot in the neck. The plasma slug had severed the carotid artery.

Lieutenant Lam never stood a chance.

As I kneeled beside him, Nashumi and her second, Bosha, moved into the room, weapons drawn. They absorbed their weapons as their helmets slipped away. Both were taken mightily by the sight.

"I called for medical response." Nashumi dropped down beside me. "It's going to take a while."

Elora nodded solemnly. She guided Raibous over to Bosha. "Take the Ensign out to the deck and make him as comfortable as you can, please. See if you can get him to talk."

Bosha guided the boy out, speaking to him softly. Raibous kept his head down and struggled to keep up with her. He was still lost in his horror.

Elora came to kneel beside me so we could get Taito out as well.

"C'mon, Lieutenant. We need to get you out of here, too. Let Elora take Lam."

Taito resisted at first, pulling Lam tighter to him.

"You've got to let him go, sweetie. We need to get you checked out."

Taito stared up at me and slowly came around. He nodded, helping to set Lam in Elora's arms. She hoisted Lam up reverently and removed him from the room.

"Are you sure you're not injured?" I asked.

"Yeah, I'm good. It's just that my legs are asleep."

I helped him stretch his legs out to get the circulation flowing. "Can you tell me what happened?"

"I don't know. I was back here making tea when they attacked. When I ran out Nalwist and Lam were already down. Raibous was returning fire as I came in, so I grabbed a plasma rifle from the safe and helped drive them back. That's when I pushed you. When the return fire eased up we grabbed Lam and dragged him back here."

Tears fell from Taito's eyes. "He was screaming. I didn't have anything back here to give him for the pain. The med kit out front had been destroyed in the barrage. All I could do was hold him."

I helped Taito to his feet and pulled him close.

“Why did they attack here? It doesn’t make any sense.”

I shook my head as I started walking him toward the door. “Ashron had been working on an escape ship for them. They were trying to access the flight bay downstairs.”

Taito scowled. He shook his head. “If I’d have known that I’d have opened it for them. I’d have spaced every damn one of them.”

As I got him out to the repair bay a response team finally pushed into the room. I sat Taito down on a grease bucket and turned him over to the medics.

“I’ll be back.”

Taito nodded, holding on to my hand for a brief second longer before letting me go.

Nashumi’s platoon had the hybrids corralled in a circle between them. I noticed the Marines had yet to arrive, too.

Funny, that.

As I looked around at the motley bastards, I realized, if it were my boat, I would have ordered the huntresses to open fire.

Good thing that it wasn't my boat.

I moved toward Elora to bemoan that very fact when, suddenly, I got a push from Gevin. "Get back here now, I need you."

I looked up at Elora and shook my head. She activated her helmet before I could mine. We split for propulsion in a flash.

The fun, it seemed, wasn't over yet.

Chapter 20

There is an instant, an interval of an eyeblink, when a ship transitions to hyperspace where it is possible to sneak a peek into the future.

These moments pass too quickly for eyes to examine or ears to engage. They manifest as a mad jolt to the nervous system, a manic momentary occurrence of emotion. One is struck with a mood, a knowledge, which leaves a permanent impression in one's guts.

I learned to open to it in my wild youth, trusting it to gauge the outcome of battle. It worked much better in my jump bomber than on larger ships. Their bigger mass absorbed the weird energy of the threshold rupture.

I'd thought it was impossible on this ship.

Until we jumped.

And a chill scraped down the entire length of my spine.

The realization and prognosis hitting simultaneously was a hell of a shock.

I stopped dead in my tracks. I needed a second to get my shit together.

Elora and I were racing mad aft at Gevin's behest along the empty length of superstructure between decks. Elora stopped in rapid fashion and glanced over.

"Did we just jump?"

"Yes ma'am."

Elora attached herself to the wall and removed her helmet. "This can't be good."

I removed mine so she could appreciate my smirk. "Has anything been yet?"

"Nena, Elora, report," the Queen Mother chimed in my ear.

"We've been summoned to attend to the captain. The mutiny goes beyond the hybrids." Elora didn't look pleased.

"As I've been made aware," The Queen Mother sounded a bit resigned. "I need you to return Elora, the mutineers initiated this jump and left our girls stranded. We need to prepare."

"On my way." Elora shot me a warm glance before replacing her helmet and screaming off.

"Nena. Nashumi and her squad will meet you outside main propulsion. Go in slowly and camouflaged. We've received reports that Captain Toll is being held hostage. Diffuse that situation immediately and by any means necessary, quickly too if you don't mind."

As angry as I was, I couldn't help but giggle. That woman was graceful under pressure. I needed to lighten up too.

"I'm all over it, Great Mother. I'll report when our goal is met."

The Queen Mother's laughter rattled my brain. "Happy hunting."

I picked up Nashumi's position and sent the customary chirp through the com. I waited for the double chirp response before camouflaging myself to take my place among them.

I'd learned that these chirps were part of an entire language developed by the ancient huntresses to communicate while tracking game. It mimicked the chirping of a common loquacious newt native to their home. Now it was used as code over open frequencies.

I had thus far only learned enough not to get myself shot.

“What’s the situation?” I asked as I linked my armor to the squad’s.

“One of the Captain’s magisters is the mutiny’s leader. When you discovered the marine, they made their move to abduct the command staff.”

I took a deep breath drawing on the absolute calm of my sisters.

“Which magister was it?” I asked.

“The female. She has support among her staff.”

I shook my head. “Motai. She was the one I saw arguing with Viginti after the mission briefing.”

The picture was clearer but still opaque. “It was the perfect opportunity when Gevin sent the Marines to meet us.”

“You mean the ones that never arrived?” Nashumi frowned.

“Exactly. What the hell happened to them?”

“Ah, that’s easy. They’re stalking us. I sent out a scout when we left to meet you.”

I grinned. Nashumi was a keen warrior.

"So Tropa was in on it, just low on the food chain. You know I really don't regret breaking his big dumb ass."

Nashumi and the girls laughed.

"Should I have them taken out?" Nashumi's smile was infectious.

I chewed on my lip for a second considering it. "No. I have a better idea. Send that scout reinforcements, engage them and pin the bastards down somewhere. Make a big show of it. They can be the diversion that gets us on the propulsion deck."

Nashumi nodded. "Ah, a great plan. Sending them out from third squad. They're closer."

"What do we know about the propulsion deck?" I glanced around the group. "Those schematics aren't in the database."

"Actually, they are." Nashumi tilted her head and smiled. "It's just that the admiral and the captain are the only two that have access."

"And now us."

Nashumi winked. "Disana is very thorough."

"Frighteningly so." I grimaced. "Okay, let's see it."

Nashumi called up the simulacrum in the group's heads up display.

Main propulsion, in a stunning fete of engineering, was a world unto itself. It was a shielded deck floating inside a self-created vacuum chamber tethered to the hyper-wave generators' superstructure.

It was impenetrable with its drawbridge withdrawn.

As I studied the schematics, I got a hollow feeling in the pit of my stomach.

"How the hell are we getting in there?"

Nashumi tilted her head. Even with her helmet on she looked disappointed.

"No problems, only puzzles and solutions."

I nodded, slowly exhaling my exasperation. "So, what's the solution?"

Nashumi shifted on her feet. I assumed she was giving the hologram a good once over.

"Crossing the vacuum isn't a problem."

Nashumi finally replied. "But we won't be able to breach the door without breaking the seal. The drawbridge is the pressure barrier."

Nashumi shifted again flowing through the view. “Ah, check this out.”

Several hatches at the bottom of the propulsion sphere started glowing. “The compressors for the heat exchangers have their own maintenance hatches and airlocks. They can be activated from both sides. They must use pressure suits to service them.”

“Interesting.” I stared at the schematics in awe. Nashumi analyzed the data as if she’d written it. She was a formidable being and a real sweetheart. “Do they generate heat? I assume they keep them in vacuum for a reason.”

“Not nearly as much as the exchangers themselves.” Nashumi scrolled thermal readings at the bottom of the image. “Our armor could withstand it long enough to access the hatch.”

I looked at the data again carefully. It was tricky but not impossible.

“Okay. I’m all for it. We have a few things to flesh out but it’s a start. We need the Queen Mother in the loop. She can coordinate with the loyalists, let them know what’s coming.”

“I’m on it.” Nashumi nodded smartly.

After the better part of an hour spent orchestrating our opus, we were ready to jam. Nashumi masterfully arranged the final pieces. She was a natural leader. Her girlies trusted her implicitly. And Nashumi loved them all as children. She was fiercely proud.

We moved forward en masse to a point just above the balcony of the tram station via the inner hull. Propulsion was the end of the line for the tram, so the promenade had an extra egress walkway at the end of the line.

It was a great place to get caught in a crossfire.

Nashumi's second, Bosha, launched a wave of nano probes. They drifted down into the station like a swarm of amoeba gnats scanning the layout.

"There isn't anyone here." I toggled over to thermal imaging on the feed from the swarm to see if there was something we'd missed.

"Have them scan for EM too," I told Bosha.

"They may have it booby trapped."

Bosha nodded, working the probes.

"Hopefully they're short staffed." Nashumi frowned. "The girls have been thinning the herd for hours now."

“Let’s hope so. We could have this wrapped up by first meal.”

Nashumi bumped my shoulder as we set off to descend. “I like the way you think, lady.”

I grinned inside my helmet. “Right back at you, sweetie.”

We stayed a few dozen meters behind the nano droids as they mapped our path. It was eerily silent. The scans showed nothing ahead of us, but I couldn’t shake the feeling that we weren’t alone.

We eased our invisible way up to the observation deck as Bosha fanned the probes out around it. Propulsion was different than the rest of the ship in that it didn’t have its offices or training facilities housed in the outer hull. Everything was contained inside the vacuum facility.

The observation deck, which looked out over the mile long outer shell of the propulsion facility, rested atop the union of the ship’s superstructure and the megastructure of the pulse drive and wave engines that rested glowing beyond in vacuum.

It was a breathtaking view.

The captain and his captors were in the observation dome above the deck. Steps rose to the dome from both sides in a grand sweeping arch. It left a lot of open ground to cross before it could be breached.

We stopped short of the deck and let the probes scan the scene. Finally, as they drifted across to the far side, they scanned a group of armed hybrids hiding near the entrance to the facility.

Nashumi led us up over the steps to creep along the ground toward them. The invisible shield worked best when it wasn't in line of sight, especially up close. We moved silently forward watching them through the lens of the nano probes.

We moved within two meters without them being aware. It made sense. Hybrids weren't very quick on the uptake with unfamiliar data. They were on the lookout for a frontal assault. They couldn't sense what they couldn't see. That was the difference.

And a bloody huge tactical advantage.

The girls dispatched the hybrids silently, uncloaking to cover their mouths as they deployed the pulse weapons directly to their temples. They dropped into their arms to be piled up in a corner out of view.

Their placement, for once, was fortuitous. We were able to have Bosha's assault team depart first and get to their breach points. Then we could assault both groups simultaneously. We couldn't risk the hybrids jumping the ship again.

Disana's key codes arrived right on time and cycled the entry system silently. Bosha's squad set out nice and safe across the void. The rest of us sat rapt, hidden in the shadows, watching them make their way across.

It took a good bit of finesse navigating the negative space to the propulsion sphere. The girlies handled it with an easy grace. They slipped inside the compressor hatches with little trouble and activated the pressurization routine without setting off the alarm.

Disana's ability to sidestep Union technology was frightening.

I was glad the Queen Mother kept a close eye on her.

After a few painful minutes spent imagining everything that could go wrong, Bosha finally signaled she was ready. I hopped up off my dead ass and cast my doubts aside. It was go time. I was here to free Gevin. Nothing was getting in the way of that.

We spread out around the tower and set ourselves to strike from multiple fronts. The people in the tower showed no signs of alarm. Zari thermal imaging was sharp enough to tell us if they had a gun or bubble gum in their pockets. We weren't going in blind.

The hybrids had the hostages bound and sat in a semi-circle near the far edge of the dome.

Anything that was on its feet was a target.

We split up our targets, each member superimposing their crest over the face of their target. Since I didn't have a crest, I drew a smiley face on mine. A series of suppressed giggles chimed along the com until Nashumi shut it down, shaking her head.

"Go!"

We raced up the steps still cloaked waiting until the last possible nanosecond to launch ourselves into the dome. We shunted power from shields to initiate a catapult response in our boots. We vaulted into the dome at an insane speed and appeared out of nowhere. The mutineers were totally taken off guard. Most fell before we even landed.

I saved mine for after my dismount.

I landed solidly behind Magister Motai as she attempted to sneak off. She stopped dead in her tracks waiting for the hammer to fall.

"I'm not going to shoot you in the back. You're going to turn around and look at me."

Motai raised her hands before turning on her heel to face me. She was human with a bit of Bituin mixed in. Her olive skin had a faint opalescence like Bituin scales. Her eyes had that cold-blooded Bituin stare as well. She was a striking woman.

It wasn't hard to see how she rallied those fuck stick Marines to her cause.

Nashumi rushed up beside me resting her hand on my shoulder. The room had been cleared. Then, just as quickly, she took off across the dome with the others to free the hostages leaving me alone with the magister.

"Ah, Commander Videt. It's nice to see you again."

"Too bad I can't say the same."

Motai snorted, expressing her derision. "Just as I'd expect of a heathen Janusian. No manners."

Now at this point you'd have thought I would have just shot the twat and gotten it over with. But, to my own surprise, I found this dumb whore amusing.

"Oh, wait. Wait a second. I get it. You're about to go all moral high ground on me, aren't you?"

The look on Motai's face was priceless. I was spot on.

I nodded slowly, my expression darkening as I stepped forward to force her back. "You're one of those holier-than-thou snot nosed Ganivet magisters, aren't you? The ones with a copy of the Tenets tucked in your panties and a joystick in your ass. I took a lot of shit from you bitches when I passed through there."

It was in that second Motai fully realized her life was in danger. She took another few steps back, looking up at me. "We've lost our way, Commander. You must know this. Nothing good can come of this plan. Any society that evolves from this will be forever tainted."

"Oh please, spare me your pious bullshit. The Tenets aren't worth the crystal they're etched in if no one is around to adhere to them. The question you should be asking is, are they worth preserving? And what are you willing to do to ensure that?"

Motai's face looked like it was about to collapse in on itself. "But the word..."

"Is only good if there's someone still around to speak the language. It's fleeting. Like everything else in the Universe."

I don't know if this blew her mind or not, but she did finally shut up.

Gevin rushed up beside me looking very much worse for the wear. He had a mad gleam seething in his clear green eyes. Before I could open my mouth, he shoved Motai away from me and shot her point blank in the head.

She hit the deck in a twisted heap.

I glared at Gevin, wide-eyed. "I wasn't done talking to her yet."

"Well, I was done with her," Gevin growled. "And it's my ship."

"Roger that."

I turned and gave Nashumi a wide-eyed glance.

Knowing him as well as I did, I knew the betrayal hurt a lot worse than the beating.

He glanced around the room, checking on his people. He looked like he'd aged decades. There was something different about his whole vibe.

"Do we have control of propulsion?"

Nashumi stepped forward. "They control the operations deck, but there are still holdouts resisting."

Gevin nodded, grimly. "Take the rest of your squad and shut them down, quickly. We must get this ship out of the open."

I winked at Nashumi before she ran off to rally the troops.

"What do you need me to do?"

Gevin's look was cold. I knew the expression.

"We need to see the Admiral." Gevin furrowed his brow. "I have a plan."

Chapter 21

The scores of bodies strewn about the ship was disturbing to witness.

I'd seen carnage in my time. But this...was beyond words.

It looked very much like a portend of the final defeat of the Union itself. The hybrids were created to represent all its varied races and genders. Now they'd become a mirror society wasn't prepared to stare into.

They were sentient. They deserved better. Seeing them this way I couldn't help but mourn. The misguided souls back home that created this mess may well find themselves in this same position soon.

When word gets out, they'll be forced to contend with an already entrenched enemy as well as one festering on their borders.

The odds looked really, really, long.

Gevin made a ship-wide announcement detailing the elimination of the saboteurs in propulsion and the execution of Magister Motai. He didn't mince words. He made them painfully aware that they'd been defeated. He called for them to stand down and they did.

In the immediate aftermath I finally got to nab a decent shift's sleep while Gevin and the admiral assessed the damage and plotted a course forward.

I didn't envy them their task.

As I made my way to blue sector to meet with the Queen Mother, I saw that cleanup crews had been formed to clear the dead.

There had been significant losses to the troops as well, especially in the first few moments when most were taken by surprise. It was a haunting sight, watching as our troops were placed reverently in body bags to be carried away on litter while the hybrid bodies were tossed haplessly on anti-gravity carts to be shot out of the nearest airlock.

It was wrong.

I arrived to discover that Gevin was meeting with the Queen Mother in her private chamber.

I stood around for a few strained moments waiting to be shown inside. The wait gave me plenty of time to imagine all manner of crazy things. The bad feeling in my gut from the last jump still lingered. I felt off balance.

Bosha finally came out of the Queen's chamber. She smiled when she saw me. "They wish you to join them."

"How long have they been in there?"

"A couple of hours." Bosha smiled, taking my hand. "The captain arrived just before midday."

"Wow. That's heavy. I wonder what's up."

"I was not privy." Bosha smiled. "I guess they wanted to run it by you first."

I raised an eyebrow, grinning, as she left me at the door.

"Ah, Commander, how are you feeling? Please take a seat." The Queen Mother's voice filled the room.

I bowed graciously, then stepped forward, waving Gevin off from rising from his chair.

"What can I do to help?"

Gevin turned to face me as I sat down. I couldn't read his expression.

It made me worry.

"The Queen Mother and I have been enjoying a very frank conversation about current events. And, as you can imagine, your name popped up."

"Oh yeah?" I smirked, easing back in my chair. "Do tell."

The Queen Mother's raspy giggle bolstered me.

Gevin wasn't amused. "We've been discussing Viginti's vivisection."

"I still can't imagine what they thought they'd learn by removing her central cortex."

Gevin wasn't pleased but followed me down the rabbit hole. "I suspect it was only for effect. They wanted us to know they were aware of her having been altered. You should have told me what you were up to."

"As I told you, Captain. Commander Videt was acting under my orders per my agreement with the admiral. I appreciate that you two are close, but this needed to be handled delicately."

Gevin sneered. "And that worked out amazingly well."

Damn. He was even more bent than I thought.

The Queen Mother's eyes flashed at the impertinence. To Gevin's great credit his expression never changed. I was impressed.

"It is true. Viginti was discovered. But the mechanism is still unclear. Dwelling on it is a waste of time at this point. We need to deal with the problem at hand."

"We have a new problem?" I raised my hands.

"Yay!"

No wonder I was summoned.

Gevin and the Queen Mother both stopped to look at me. The Queen Mother nodded her appreciation. Gevin's lack of expression was telling.

"The admiral, in his infinite wisdom, has decided to allow anyone that wants to abdicate their position passage back to Union space. All remaining hybrids are ordered to leave."

"Wow. That's a bold move. Is he sure he'll have anyone left?"

Gevin frowned and looked away. I was really on his nerves now. It made me a little sad.

"We have a good idea now which personnel were involved in the mutiny. They will be asked to decide, discommendation or death. And that will be the end of it."

"And I take it you don't agree."

Gevin's eyes flashed. The answer was clear.

"So how are we sending them away? You're not planning on giving up the other destroyer?"

Gevin's frown deepened. "We've amended our battle plan to compensate. Unfortunately, in this new scenario we are going to need you to fly two more missions for hyper matter."

I let the news fully sink in before I opened my mouth. It was a lot to swallow.

"So how long are you planning on staying here? I thought our ass was in the breeze."

Gevin's glance was heavy. "With a hard wind is blowing, Commander. We can only risk another twenty-four hours. The destroyer is being prepared for departure as we speak. As soon as it makes hyper-space I want you out. That will give you a few hours rest between jumps barring complications."

I scoffed. "Didn't work so good the first time."

"And we've made allowances, Commander. Just make sure you're ready."

"No problem," I shrugged. "You just let me know when you're ready."

I climbed out of my chair and bolted for the door without being dismissed.

"Where are you going?" Gevin detested protocol breaches.

At that moment, I didn't care. I'd earned one.

"To hop in the simulator. I want to be prepared."

Gevin didn't reply. I didn't give him a chance.

I made my way up to the tech deck battling my own hot-headed nature. I understood how upset Gevin was. He'd been betrayed. But he needed to rein it in. Especially where I was concerned. After everything I'd done for him, after everything I'd done since boarding this flying madhouse, it hurt.

It was a bad sign. We were all on edge. This mission really was for all the marbles. The situation had shown itself to be that dire.

Unfortunately, everyone was unraveling behind it.

The main tech deck was still a mess of bodies when I arrived. I hadn't called ahead so I wasn't sure if anyone was even there. I felt bad that I hadn't checked in on Taito or poor little Raibous. If they weren't here, I would have seen them before I went to work.

I climbed down the steps to the shot-up shell of the division office. As I reached the door, I got the feeling I wasn't alone. I donned my helmet and started scanning.

Raibous was cowering in the shadows in the back room.

I wept.

I removed my helmet and stepped inside. "Come on out, Ensign. It's me. Nena."

"Commander?" Raibous stepped out of the shadows looking mightily relieved.

"What are you doing down here? You can't be on duty."

"I'm not. I've been relieved until first watch to-morrow. I just couldn't lay around the rack. I had to do something."

"So, you came here?

Raibous nodded gently. He walked past me through the door to sit on the step. I stepped out and joined him.

The view was disturbing.

"I needed to see this." Raibous peered out at the carnage like he was seeing his last sunset. "I couldn't expect not to. We're too far gone now. Win or lose this boat will never make it back to port."

My heart dropped. I wanted to tell him he was wrong. I couldn't.

I could only sugar coat it.

"Never say never, Ensign. Look at me, I've been ass deep in this war since it started and I'm still here."

Raibous smiled. "Yeah, but you're a complete maniac. Death's afraid to call on you."

I got a raucous laugh out of that. The ensign had a quick wit.

"Perhaps, but the Universe only fosters a fool for so long. The rest is, I don't know, luck, fate, providence? Beats the hell out of me. I'm just learning to be grateful for all my mornings, however many are left."

Something stirred in Raibous' placid silver eyes. He nodded, considering it. "Thank you, Commander. That helps."

"Good, I'm glad. You can't control what the day throws at you. You can only control your reaction."

Raibous nodded absently, lost in thought. I couldn't begin to imagine where his mind was.

I wept for the future these kids would have to endure. If they managed to survive.

Win or lose the Union will never be what it was. If at all ever again. These kids will be left with nothing but the shell of a once great idea.

Hopefully, eventually, they'll build something better.

"What do you miss most about home?"

Raibous' question almost went right by me as I was lost in my own head.

"What do I miss about home?" I closed my eyes and took a deep breath. "I miss the scent of magenta lilies filling my room on a breezy summer morning. I can still smell them if I think about it hard enough. That to me is home. What about you?"

Raibous smiled faintly. “I miss my friends. I miss all the crazy stuff we used to do.”

I grinned. “Were you a wild child?”

Raibous giggled. “Have you met me? No, I was never in any serious trouble or anything. My friends and I used to build rover drones and play chicken with them out on the lava fields. It was dangerous being out there and risking getting caught in a blowout. So, we made the drones explore where it was extremely dangerous. I lost more than a couple of them over the edge.”

“That does sound kind of fun. Did you ever build a flyer?”

“Flyers are expensive. And they don’t do well with all the heat and convection currents above the fields. I knew a couple of guys that spent big money on them only to have them meltdown on their first flight. That was hilarious.”

Raibous’ smile faded slowly. He looked up into my eyes as tears ran down his face. His expression broke my heart.

“Commander, I want to go home.”

I pulled Raibous close and let him cry on my shoulder.

I couldn't not. It was a maternal instinct. And truthfully, at that point, I was ready to go with him.

I wanted to tell him about the admiral's plan but thought better of it. They wanted rid of the mutineers and hybrids not shell-shocked ensigns. It was better just to let it go.

"I can dig it, kid, one hundred percent. But you must consider that you might not like what you find there. I guarantee it's not going to be as it was when you left. The situation is dire everywhere. You just might be in the safest place."

Raibous shook his head as he sat up. "Well, now that is depressing. But I take your meaning. And here is the only place where I can really help."

"Now you're catching on. I knew you were a bright kid. Now go on back to your rack and get some rest. Put one some tunes and zone out for a while. Forget about all this and just be."

Raibous smiled, standing to salute. "Thanks, Commander. I appreciate it."

I smiled returning his salute. "Hey, I'm only really doing this for myself, you know. You're my new ground crew. I need you on point tomorrow."

Raibous grinned from ear to ear. "For you, Commander, anything. I'll see you then."

I let him drop down a couple of steps before I yelled, "And bring coffee. The office is a mess."

I got a genuine laugh out of him with that. It put a smile on my face.

If you're purposely driving over the edge of a cliff, you might as well smile.

Chapter 22

Grey sector, where the remaining destroyer, *Vodyn,* docked looked exactly like my second home in blue sector only in reverse and about two kilometers away. The two destroyers docked on opposite sides of the ship along the aft outer hull. When linked to the ship they provided additional firepower and maneuvering propulsion.

With the *Mojyn* lost the balance was gone

Now, the *Vodyn's* sat empty awaiting a strange fate. It had been repurposed to be a ship of exile. I couldn't see the sense of losing a perfectly good weapon to the task. But Kirpich knew something I didn't. Sending it home to central command could have been a necessary precaution. The fleet could use all the firepower they could muster.

Now, as the prisoners were led in to meet that fate, grey sector became a mob scene.

Admiral Kirpich, for whatever lunatic reason, chose to have an open forum to pass judgment on the mutineers and broadcast their exile ship wide.

The training center was filled beyond capacity with more queued up to file in. There were so many that I was beginning to wonder if anyone was left on watch. As I looked around, I figured there really wasn't any need to broadcast the damn thing. Everyone was already here.

I enjoyed a catbird seat while attending to the Queen Mother. Nashumi and I were loitering behind the dais taking in the whole mad scene.

Bosha's squad was chosen to guard the mutineers. They were segregated to one side of the hall and seated in rows on the floor. There had to be close to two hundred of them. They had come extremely close to being wiped out completely, especially the hybrids.

The consensus from the crowd was that they should have been.

Elora ordered the girls to keep their helmets on and weapons drawn. The vibe in the room was charged. As many as were present it wouldn't take much for them to riot.

The girls were perfectly intimidating as they loomed over their charges. Pure fear kept them docile.

The admiral strolled in, finally, with Gevin and the *Vodyn's* skipper, Commander Gester in tow. All of them had this weird hollow look in their eyes. It was disquieting.

I didn't know if it was something they'd discussed or their reaction to the situation at hand, but it was jarring.

I looked away trying not to catch Gevin's eye. I focused on the crowd. He was still pissed at me, and I was trying my best not to care.

Kirpich approached the podium with grim determination. He looked more haggard than the last time I'd seen him. This mission was eating him alive and it was starting to show.

"Order in the gallery!" Kirpich's voice, however, was deep, loud, and clear. "Let's bring this thing to order."

The crowd slowly fell silent. The hybrids turned their full attention to the admiral to avoid the murderous gaze of the crew.

I did notice one older human crewman up front among the mutineers staring at the crowd. He looked genuinely mystified by their rage. His expression stirred my heart.

I had to remember that some of these poor souls were just worn out. This gentleman looked well past mandatory retirement age. He shouldn't even be on the boat. Naval reserves were worse than I'd realized.

I didn't know what he'd done but it reeked of desperation.

"I called you all together today to witness the execution of sentence for those found guilty of mutiny against this ship and its command. It is also my intention to advise and update you on our mission moving forward."

That caused a stir in the gallery.

"This mission has been hard on all of us. We find ourselves at a crossroads. One for which we could never hope to adequately prepare. But it does my heart good to see you here today after having witnessed your courage and your commitment to duty and to this ship. After seeing this, in vivid detail, it's my promise to do better about keeping you informed on what we're facing out there. These next few weeks will not be easy. But I am confident that together we will be able to see it through."

The applause surprised me. I'm not sure why. With all the uncertainty looming on the horizon these folks needed something to believe in. It was apparent the bulk of the crew was with him, and he had the good sense to build on that.

"Now, to our first order of business, execution of sentence. I want to go on the record by saying that this was a most difficult decision and one that we did not arrive at lightly. Captain Toll and I had a most spirited debate about this. And though the Tenets are clear on the fate of mutineers we find ourselves in unprecedented times."

Another row passed through the crowd. They weren't crazy about it but seemed willing to defer to the admiral's wisdom.

"In this instance exile is preferable. Without benefit of communication on this mission I believe it imperative that the Admiralty learn about the danger posed by the series twenty hybrids."

That garnered a lively reaction. Kirpich had them in his pocket now.

"And if the home space is threatened, this lot will be there to stick their necks out for their homes."

The crowd murmured. It was practical but not preferred.

Kirpich turned and glanced at Gevin, who still looked bothered. Kirpich's gaze had made it worse.

Gevin was seething.

Something was up. There was something going on between them.

In that silent interval the older gentleman I'd spotted earlier rose. "May I speak before the sentence is passed? It is my right."

The crowd went crazy.

I was struck by the wounded expression on the man's face as the crew tried to shout him down. One of Bosha's girls moved to block him, stun baton extended. The old gentleman flinched when she approached.

I was behooved to raise my voice when the Queen Mother vaulted out of her chair. She landed out in front of the dais between the two groups. She slammed her staff into the deck and snarled at the crowd.

"Silence! He will be allowed to speak!"

Her voice resonated through the hall like thunder. Behind her Bosha's troops closed ranks and marched forward ready to protect her and the prisoners.

The display quickly convinced everyone to shut up.

I grinned from ear to ear as Nashumi and I leapt to her side.

Admiral Kirpich held up his hands unsettled by the scene. “Please. It is his right.”

A few hushed murmurs swept through the crowd but not many. They stood in awe of the Queen Mother as she stepped aside.

The man stepped forward slowly. He glanced sidelong at the Zari before moving to stand before the admiral.

“Admiral, Queen Mother, thank you for allowing me to speak. I want you to know, sir, that I have the utmost respect for you. But I could not in good faith go forward ignoring my duty to the Tenets. You see, sir, it was my task to cull the brains from these sentient creatures to coordinate the drones. I couldn’t do it. What has been perpetrated on these beings is wrong. A message had to be sent. And I regret it had to be so.”

The old man turned and faced the crowd. There were angry faces abounding, but they didn’t speak up.

“We have forgotten that we stand on the shoulders of great beings. We are the legacy of the Paladin Aleph. Beings who surfed the stars as giants! Now all these many centuries later we pale in their grand tradition. What would they say of us now?

Here in our darkest hour, we have abandoned our principles. The Navy I joined in my youth is no more and may well never be again. I never thought I'd live to see it. I accept my fate with a clear conscience. I hope you all can do the same."

The man dropped his head and returned to his place with the other prisoners. The expression of sorrow on his face was genuine and quite profound. I was glad that he would be allowed to live and at least have a fighting chance at home. It was more than some of them deserved.

Up on the dais Gevin was shaking with rage. I didn't understand his reaction. It was a harsh assessment but not patently untrue.

"Sergeant-at-arms, I want that man detained."

Huh?

Gevin's voice dripped with rage. He was usually so reserved as to be unflappable. I didn't understand what was going on with him.

Kirpich didn't either. He whipped his head around to glare at Gevin. I couldn't hear what he said in reply as the crowd sounded off once again.

The sergeant-at-arms looked around, perplexed. He started forward but looked leery about walking past the Zari. He glanced up at Gevin in disbelief.

"I want him taken to the brig, now, Sergeant," Gevin's voice seethed. "Stay with him until I arrive."

I started to step forward, but the Queen Mother tapped her staff gently down between my feet. I looked at her sidelong to see her shake her head subtly. We were staying out of this one.

The crowd didn't know how to react as the sergeant took the man by the arm and led him away. I was right there with them. I didn't understand what the hell was going on, or what had gotten into Gevin.

All I knew was I was staying away from the son of a bitch. He was starting to lose it.

After they were gone, Admiral Kirpich, who didn't look especially pleased by the turn of events, held up his hands to settle the crowd. "Let us commit our foe to their fate and be done with it. Get them off my ship."

The Queen Mother chirped Bosha into action. The Huntresses got the prisoners on their feet and herded toward the airlock. It wasn't until then that I caught sight of my old buddy, former Gunnery Sergeant Tropa. He must have been skulking in the back of the group trying to hide from me.

He saw me as one of Bosha's girls gave him a nudge. Never in all my years have I had someone look at me with so much hate. If it had been any other sentient in the universe, it might have bothered me.

I hoped he would see me wink before he was shoved away. I think it would be a good memory for him.

The crowd remained silent as the mutineers were spirited away. A lot wished they could tag along. But bravery is pushing your fear aside and doing your duty. This crew had demonstrated that admirably. They were willing to face whatever was coming their way.

After a few long minutes of jabbering amongst ourselves, a hologram of the *Vodyn* undocking appeared in the middle of the room. It powered out a few thousand kilometers before turning perpendicular to the gravity well to jump, a weird course given Aknowi's unique position. Something about it bothered me.

After the ship jumped the hologram faded and the admiral returned to the podium.

There was a moment, a quick flash in the admiral's eyes as he looked out at the crowd, where he looked completely unsure of himself. If it wasn't self-doubt, it was worse.

I glanced over at the Queen Mother again to see if she saw it too. She put her hand on my shoulder and leaned in, "Let it go."

I raised an eyebrow in response. Something about this whole damn thing was off. And I'd been left out of the loop.

I didn't like it.

"The next phase of our mission will commence in exactly twenty-six hours. Our target is the Aratani stronghold at Zuridan."

Zuridan? Really?

"Our plan is to use our hypermatter reserves to strike key enemy targets and throw them into disarray. Task forces from the main fleet will enter the systems in our wake and mop up. Once we hit Zuridan we will be moving on to Tannakye and then Mostele. Our plan is not to get mired down but contingency plans have been created in case we are forced to engage. It's a hit and run mission folks and if we play our cards right, we just might get out of it with our asses intact."

By this point I was completely mystified. What happened to hitting Aratan?

Gevin had finally gotten through to him. But if that were true, you'd figure he wouldn't be so bloody grouchy.

All these things in pieces didn't add up.

The crowd quieted in reflection. I don't think they quite knew what to make of the reversal. It was good news. It was a hell of a lot safer than sacking Aratan. I just couldn't fathom how we got here.

"If events follow our design, we will be docked for refit on Ganivet in ninety days."

That drew a cheer from the crowd. An end was in sight.

I wasn't sure if I bought it or not. Something was off. Something felt wrong in my gut.

"You're C.O.'s have your assignments and will fill you in on the details. I just wanted you to hear it from me first. I trust this mission to your capable hands. Now, let's get to work. Dismissed."

The Queen Mother returned to her seat on the dais as the crowd sauntered out. I followed her up and took my place behind her. As I did, Nashumi filed out with Bosha's squad, no doubt at the Queen Mother's urging.

Gevin returned to his seat as well after a brief conversation with Commander Gester who left as well. His face was drawn, grave. I'd never seen him displaying emotion. Now sorrow radiated like a beacon.

Admiral Kirpich sat down next to Gevin, swiping at his leg as he dropped. The two exchanged glances of what I can only describe as bewilderment. They were searching for something in each other's eyes. I got the impression neither saw what they sought.

The vibe in the room was heavy.

I stood by quietly as the last of the crew filed out and waited until Kirpich dismissed the guards to post outside.

"Okay, so who wants to tell me what in the actual fuck is going on?"

I moved to the Queen Mother's side so I could see her face. I figured she'd be the one to answer.

"The *Vondyn* isn't headed for Ganivet." Gevin rose from his chair and moved close to look me in the eye. "It's headed for Aratan's primary."

There are very few times in one's life when a revelation occurs that rattles both mind and body. When they do, they are deep and abiding. This one hit hard.

"You sent them on a one-way ride to Ara in a hypermatter bomb? Are you kidding me right now?"

Gevin's eyes dropped. This went against everything he was raised to believe. He was in agony. That's what I'd been seeing. He was ashamed it had to come to this.

Kirpich's face reddened. He opened his mouth to speak but the Queen Mother cut him off.

"The mutineers were the authors of their own fate, Nena. They knew the punishment was death. We could not let it be for nothing. There's too much at stake."

On a purely practical tactical level it was genius.

By the Tenets it was blasphemous.

"This was carefully crafted." Kirpich's expression was stern. "The prisoners will never know what hit them. It will be an easy death and better than they deserve. And we give the lives of this crew, who never faltered in their duty, a shot at a real future. I was able to give them hope where there was none. I could do nothing else."

I couldn't argue his logic. It was an able move for someone with their back against the wall. He put the lives of his crew above the framework of his beliefs, he and Gevin. Both were honorable men in my eyes.

History could make its own decision.

"So, you saved the life of that crewman just now." I glanced at Gevin.

Gevin nodded, looking as if a great weight had been dropped from his shoulders. "At least temporarily. We will investigate his role in this further. If dereliction is his only offense it will be a rip on his record not a death sentence. He was standing on the core of his beliefs. I can't fault him for that."

I nodded. "It's hard to walk a straight line when you're mired in chaos. We should rejoice that there's still a few of you out there."

That put a smile on Gevin's face albeit briefly. "Heathen."

"You wouldn't want me any other way."

Kirpich rose from his seat clapping his hands together. "Well, Commander, now that you've been read in above your paygrade, are you ready to make these next two drops?"

I glanced at the admiral, managing a grin. "Far be it from me to shirk my duty, sir. Let's get this war wagon powered up."

It was time for this to end.

Chapter 23

Taito and Raibous were hard at work preparing the dropship when I arrived on deck. I stopped at the top of the steps and took a second to watch them. I'd grown fond of both. With everything whirring through my head about this drop, I wanted to make sure I remembered to enjoy every second I had with them.

On this mission nothing was a given.

The main lab was slowly returning to order as maintenance drones worked to repair the offices and the damage done in the hanger. The crews on the top deck were already back to a full shift.

The new orders were for ordinance. The hit and run tactic required special ordinance for the hyper matter weapons. Taito scaled down the original design for application against star bases and capital ships. If I could complete two more runs it would be possible to power hundreds of these small yield devices. More than enough to thwart the Aratani remanent.

But to ponder victory now would be to misunderstand where we were. Beyond this point a whole new stage of being awaited. The consequences, ramifications and repercussions thereof are impossible to ponder. It was best now to just take a deep breath and live in the moment. It was the only thing to trust as true.

"It's about time you got here." Taito smiled as I approached. "I was about to put Raibous here in a flight suit."

Raibous' double take induced a fit of giggles. They were both quick witted scamps and great guys. They'll make a hell of a team.

"I don't think he has quite enough boobs to fill out one of mine."

Taito barely kept a straight face. "I was going to have him stuff it from the bog roll."

I lost it. I hadn't laughed that hard in years. It was great to just laugh. I laughed even harder when Raibous blushed blue.

"Are you ready to do this thing, Commander?" Taito wrapped me in a hug as I hopped up on the skirt platform.

"As ready as I'm going to get, I guess. I just want to be done. Then I can see if Gevin will transfer me to the kitchens now that all the hybrids are gone."

Taito grinned. "Do you know how to cook?"

"No, but it'll be nice and sedate.

"You know you aren't getting off that easy."

I rolled my eyes. "I know but you can let a girl dream."

Taito chuckled. "Sorry. That's my bad."

"Do human females dream differently than the males?" Raibous asked.

I got a great giggle out of that.

"Yes, we do, ensign. We dream big, expensive, and lavish."

Taito winked at Raibous. "Truer words were never spoken."

The perplexed look on Raibous' face set me giggling again.

It was a most welcome distraction from the whirlwind in my head.

We settled into the preflight, still talking and laughing. And we still managed to have the ship ready ahead of schedule.

Slim was all fired up and in the middle of telling a dirty joke when the Queen Mother stepped inside followed by both the admiral and Gevin.

I think Slim fried the circuitry shutting down his blowhole.

Their visit made me worry. As if it were the final chance to see the impending corpse.

Did I mention I was an optimist?

“Ah, Commander. Good. We were told you were set to go.”

I rolled off the flight couch to greet them. “Yes ma’am. I’m just waiting on the flight boss.”

The Queen wrapped me up in a big hug. It didn’t do a thing to bolster my feelings on the matter.

“I’d be a fool to try and tell you I wasn’t worried.” The Queen Mother smiled. “But if anyone can pull this off, it’s you, girlie. I didn’t train you to be a huntress because of your looks, you know.”

I couldn’t help but grin. “No? That makes me a little sad, I think.”

“You’ll do fine.” Kirpich grinned. “We’re not shutting the Well down until you come back through it. So don’t dally long. You’ve got another drop to go.”

"Yeah, I'm not looking to repeat that either. I'll be back as quickly as possible. I want the captain to have time to prepare me a decent meal before I go back."

The sly smile on Gevin's face was a welcome sight. Hopefully, he'd had some time to process his feelings. "I don't remember agreeing to that."

I grinned. "Yeah, well, I'm not surprised. You were a little preoccupied with the mutiny and all."

The look on his face was priceless. "Really? Well in that case it must be true. I was a bit preoccupied. So, what would you like to have my honored guest?"

"V rations and a good bottle of wine."

That got a good laugh out of everyone.

"Let's save the wine for after the second drop." The Admiral grinned. "It'll be on me."

I smiled, leaning in to kiss him on the cheek. "Well, now I am in a hurry. Let's get this show on the road. Call the flight boss and tell him to get his shit together. You know his C.O., right?"

Laughter filled the tiny ship. I cherished every second of it.

Knowing these five people changed my life for the better, however long it lasted. No matter what happened this experience was worthy of my time and the twisted path that ushered me here.

I wouldn't change it for the world. Hopefully, it will continue.

I strapped myself into the command couch of the dropship still smiling from my visit. I felt a lot better about my odds. I was bolstered by their belief, and I felt totally on top of my game.

So, as the ship powered up around me, I counted my blessings. There were far more than I ever realized.

"We are at full power, Commander. The ship is yours."

I bit my lip as I assumed control. "You ready to do this, Slim?"

"Once more into the breach, Commander, let's hope we don't get stuck."

I smiled as I deactivated the docking clamp. "That's what I love about you, Slim, your unbridled optimism."

"It's nice to be noticed."

"Well sequence initiated, Commander Videt. You may begin your approach."

The voice of the flight boss sounded in my ears.

"Flight, crossing shield threshold now, confirm Well dilation."

"You are go for drop, Commander. The captain says shake a leg."

I grinned as I turned the nose of the ship toward the Well. "You tell him I'll be back in time for dinner."

Laughter lifted the flight boss's voice, "Confirmed, Commander. It's a date."

I didn't reply. I just smiled as I throttled up the wave engines and dropped.

As the quantum wake dispersed out ahead of the ship the first thing I noticed was a drastic change in condition. The density of energy that we had fought against the day before was all but gone. There were a few sparse energy waves rising to meet us but nothing that required much change in course.

"What in the hell is this? It's like we're in a whole different place."

"Yeah, this can't be good." Slim sounded flustered. "I'm trying to scan down to the level of that storm we encountered but the signal isn't returning."

I eased back on the throttle and did a spectral analysis on my own. As soon as I toggled through to the X-ray band my heart nearly stopped in my chest. The storm that we passed through had gone from something akin to a hurricane to a massive quantum singularity. All the energy that we had encountered before was being pulled into the eye.

"Slim...."

"I see it, Commander. Neutral. Engines set for reverse in three, two."

I opened our sail abreast to slow our momentum quicker. Then dropped it flipping the ship a hundred and eighty degrees on its yaw axis. As soon as I flipped the ship around, I throttled the wave engines up to full power and vectored them to a pinpoint. I detected an initial burst in forward motion, but it rapidly faded leaving us suspended, motionless. Then, as I started shutting down non-essential systems to shunt more power to the engines, the ship, ever so slowly, started losing ground.

It was an eerie moment.

The hull vibrated around me, resonating with the output of the engines. We were close to breaking apart. And, for one slow terrible second, I wondered if I shouldn't just let it happen.

"Cutting power to the engines, Commander. Reverse course, again. We're just going to have to ride this out."

"Ride it out?" My voice came out more panicked than I would have liked. I removed my helmet to peer into the reality of the cockpit. "There's no way we'll survive going into that thing. And, if we do, we'll sure as hell never make it back out."

Slim appeared beside me in the cockpit. His virtual countenance exuded calm as he gazed into my eyes. "Nena, we can do this. It's just going to take a whole big bunch of out of the box thinking. Are you with me?"

I looked at him, nodding, as I took a long deep breath. I needed to get a grip on myself. Panicking was not going to help get us out of here.

I hit the thrusters and turned the nose of the ship back toward the direction of our descent. The vibration in the hull eased as I leveled us out to surf along the inflow of energy.

Slim stayed with me in the cockpit as he calculated entry points into the eye. "The influx of energy is continuing past the surface of the singularity.

There's a hole in that thing somewhere. I think that with enough speed we can surf right along inside."

I turned to stare at him. "You do remember what happened last time, right?"

"Yes, I do, and I think that the time disruption you experienced was a phenomenon of the pressure build up. I'd be willing to bet that the time bubble collapsed when all this energy started crossing the event horizon."

I looked at Slim and smirked. "That's a whole lot of surmising you've got going on there, pal. Is any of it based on actual physics?"

Slim smiled. "Nothing that makes any sense in real space, but hyperspace is different. I think I'm starting to get a handle on it."

I started laughing loudly, slap happy from the absolute absurdity of our predicament. "Well, I'm glad you do Slim, because I'm lost."

Slim turned to me with a blank expression, "Just get ready to throttle up the wave engines, Commander. We're about to become the fastest thing in the galaxy."

"Well, that's good. No matter what happens, it'll be over quick."

I settled into my command couch and clicked my vision back over to the external cameras. The vast maw of the energy singularity looming out ahead of me was terrifying. I ignored it choosing instead to focus on my instrument readings.

"Set course for the divergence, here," Slim illuminated a tiny swirl just above the perceived equator of the singularity.

"That's not much of a hole."

"It'll grow on you." Slim highlighted the opening on the display. "I gauge it at 60 kilometers."

"Oh, well that's plenty of room, then." If I'd have been using my eyes, I'd have rolled them. "Okay, course laid in. Hold on to your circuits, Slim.

"Here we go."

I throttled up the wave engines to full power before constricting the thrust. The ship lurched forward so fast that the dampening field didn't have time to react. The sudden acceleration shoved me back onto the couch as the singularity rushed up to meet me.

Waves of charged plasma illuminated the shields as we crossed the event horizon. It took only moments before the singularity filled my vision. I held my breath as my point of entry approached. I made a few small course corrections trying to stay clear of the massive waves of energy being pulled in around me. Then, before I had a chance to react, the hole flooded with a sudden influx of energy and sealed shut dead in front of me.

There was absolutely no time to react. All I could see was my own reflection in the void.

We hit the singularity's surface at a multiple of the speed of light.

Everything, in an eyeblink, ended.

And then, later, in a dream beyond darkness...the stirring scent of magenta lilies.

About The Author

Lawrence Parlier is an author/poet/musician from Cincinnati, Ohio.

His debut novel, *Sierra Court Blues*, was released in 2013. His second novel, *The Frontman*, was published in 2020.

A lifelong musician, Parlier started playing guitar and singing for the art rock/metal band, The Malevolent, right out of high school. He has played with Cosmic Zombies, Chaos Ritual and is now fronting his new band, Flux Corporation.

He has a passion for old movies, especially classic sci-fi, horror and film noir.

www.ingramcontent.com/pod-product-compliance
Lightning Source LLC
Chambersburg PA
CBHW071410200726
48294CB00002B/343

* 9 7 8 1 9 9 8 8 0 6 6 1 4 *